愿你历尽沧桑内心安然无恙

[澳大利亚]大卫·凯恩斯 等 著
张白桦 译

世界微型小说精选
奇幻卷（中英双语）

中国国际广播出版社

图书在版编目（CIP）数据

愿你历尽沧桑　内心安然无恙：英汉对照/（澳）大卫·凯恩斯等著；张白桦译.—北京：中国国际广播出版社，2021.5
（译趣坊.世界微型小说精选）
ISBN 978-7-5078-4888-5

Ⅰ.①愿… Ⅱ.①大…②张… Ⅲ.①小小说－小说集－澳大利亚－现代－汉、英 Ⅳ.①I611.45

中国版本图书馆CIP数据核字（2021）第064475号

愿你历尽沧桑　内心安然无恙（中英双语）

著　　者	［澳大利亚］大卫·凯恩斯 等
译　　者	张白桦
策　　划	张娟平
责任编辑	笑学婧
校　　对	张　娜
设　　计	国广设计室
出版发行	中国国际广播出版社 ［010-83139469　010-83139489（传真）］
社　　址	北京市西城区天宁寺前街2号北院A座一层 邮编：100055
印　　刷	环球东方（北京）印务有限公司
开　　本	880×1230　1/32
字　　数	140千字
印　　张	7.5
版　　次	2021年6月　北京第一版
印　　次	2021年6月　第一次印刷
定　　价	35.00元

版权所有　盗版必究

代 序

微型小说界的一个奇异存在

陈春水

张白桦，女，于1963年4月出生于辽宁沈阳一个世代书香的知识分子家庭，父亲是中国第一代俄语专业大学生。她曾先后就读于三所高校，具有双专业教育背景，所修专业分别为英国语言文学、比较文学与世界文学。她有两次跳级经历，一次是从初二到高三，另一次是从大一到大二。最后学历为上海外国语大学文学硕士，研究方向为译介学，师从谢天振教授（国际知名比较文学专家与翻译理论家、译介学创始人、中国翻译学创建人、比较文学终身奖获得者），为英美文学研究专家、翻译家胡允桓（与杨宪益、沙博理、赵萝蕤、李文俊、董乐山同获"中美文学交流奖"，诺贝尔文学奖得主托妮·莫里森世界范围内研究兼汉译第一人，翻译终身奖获得者）私淑弟子。她现为内蒙古工业大学外国语学院副教授、硕士研究生导师，并兼任中国比较文学学会翻译研究会理事、上海翻译家协会会员、内蒙古作家协会会员。张白桦于1987年开始文学创作,已在《读者》《中外期刊文萃》《青年博览》《小小说选刊》《青年参考》《文学故事报》等海内外一百多种报刊,以及生活·读书·新知三联书店、中译出版社、北京大学出版社、中国国际广播出版社,公开出版以微型小说翻译为主,包括长篇小说、中篇小说、散文、随笔、诗歌、杂文、评论翻译和原创等在内的编著译作36部,累计1200万字。

在中国微型小说界,众所周知的是:以性别而论,男性译作者多,女性译作者少;以工作内容而论,搞创作的多,搞研究的少;以文学样式而论,只创作微型小说的作者多,同时创作长篇小说、散文、诗歌、文学评论的作者少;以作者性质而论,搞原创的多,搞翻译的少;以翻译途径而论,外译汉的译者多,汉译外的译者少;以译者而论,搞翻译的人多,同时搞原创的人少。而具备上述所有"少"于一身的奇异存在,恐怕张白桦是绝无仅有的一位。

张白桦是当代中国微型小说第一代译作者,也是唯一因微型小说翻译而获奖的翻译家。其译作量大质优,覆盖面广泛,风格鲜明,具有女性文学史、微型小说史意义;是中国第一个从理论上,从宏观和微观层面,论证当代外国微型小说汉译的文学史意义的学者,具有翻译文学史意义;小说创作篇幅涉及长篇、中篇、短篇、微型小说,创作的文学样式覆盖小说、散文、诗歌、文学评论等主要文学样式;是既有微型小说译作,又有微型小说原创的全能型译作家，且译作与原创具有通约性；还是微型小说英汉双向翻译的译作者。她的微型小说翻译实践开创了中国微型小说双向翻译的两个"第一"："译趣坊"系列图书为中国首部微型小说译文集，在美国出版的《凌鼎年微型小说选集》为中国首部微型小说自选集英译本。

2002年，其微型小说译著《英汉经典阅读系列散文卷》曾获上海外国语大学研究生学术文化节科研成果奖；1998年，其微型小说译作《爱旅无涯》获《中国青年报·青年参考》最受读者喜爱的翻译文学作品；她本人曾在2001年当选小小说存档作家、2002年当选为当代微型小说百家；微型小说译作《仇家》当选为全国第四次微型小说续写大赛竞赛原作；2012年，其译作《海妖的诱惑》获以色列第32届世界诗人大会主席奖等文学奖项；"译趣坊"系列图书深受广大青年读者喜欢。

此外，她的论文《外国微型小说在中国的初期接受》入选复旦大学出版社的《润物有声——谢天振教授七十华诞纪念文集》，以及湖南大学出版社的张春的专著《中国小小说六十年》续表。译作《门把手》入选春风文艺出版社出版的《21世纪中国文学大系2002年翻译文学》。译作《生命倒计时》入选春风文艺出版社出版的谢天振、韩忠良的专著《21世纪中国文学大系2010年翻译文学》。

张白桦关于外国微型小说的论文具有前沿性和开拓意义。例如，《外国微型小说在中国的初期接受》是国内对于外国微型小说在中国接受的宏观梳理和微观分析。《当代外国微型小说汉译的文学史意义》证实了"微型小说翻译与微型小说原创具有同样建构民族、国别文学发展史的意义,即翻译文学应该,也只能是中国文学的一部分"。她指出,当代外国微型小说汉译的翻译文学意义在于:"推动中国当代的主流文学重归文学性,重归传统诗学的'文以载道'的传统;引进并推动确立了一种新型的、活力四射的文学样式;当代微型小说汉译提高了文学的地位,直接催生并参与改写了中国当代文学史,以一种全新的文体重塑了当代主流诗学。"

其论文也反映出张白桦的文学翻译观和文学追求,例如,在《外国微型小说在中国的初期接受》中,她说:"吾以吾手译吾心。以文化和文学的传播为翻译的目的,以妇女儿童和青年为目标读者,让国人了解世界上其他民族的妇女儿童和青年的生存状态。以'归化'为主,'异化'为辅的翻译策略,全译为主,节译和编译为辅,突出译作的影响作用和感化作用,从而形成了简洁隽永、抒情、幽默、时尚的翻译风格。与此同时,译作与母语原创的微型小说,在思想倾向、语言要素、风格类型和审美趣味上形成了通约性和文化张力,丰富了译作的艺术表现力和感染力。"

在《当代外国微型小说汉译的文学史意义》中,她说:"文学翻译是创造性叛逆,创造性叛逆赋予原作以第二次生命。处于文学样式'真空状态'的中国第一代微型小说译者一方面充分发挥了翻译的主体性作用,挥洒着'创造性叛逆'所带来的'豪杰'范儿,对于原文和原语文化'傲娇'地'引进并抵抗着',有意和无意地遵循着自己的文学理想和审美趣味'舞蹈'着,为翻译文学披上了'中国红'的外衣,在内容和形式上赋予译作一种崭新的面貌和第二次生命。一方面在原文、意识形态、经济利益、诗学观念的'镣铐'上,'忠实'并'妥协'着。"

著名评论家张锦贻在《亭亭白桦秀译林》中说:"张白桦所译的作品范围极广,涉及世界各大洲,但选择的标准却极严,注重原作表现生活的力度和反映社会的深度。显然,张白桦对于所译原作的这种选择,绝不仅仅是出于爱好,而是反映出她的审美意识和情感倾向。她着力在译作中揭示不同地区、不同国度、不同社会、不同人种的生存境况和心理状态,揭示东西方之间的文化差异和分歧,都显示出她是从人性和人道的角度来观察现实的人生。而正是通过这样的观察,才使她能够真正地去接触各国文学中那些反映社会底层的大众作品,才能使她真正地关注儿童和青年,也才使她的译作真正地走向中国的民众。事实证明,译作的高品位必伴以译者识见的高明和高超。脱了思想内核,怕是做不好文学译介工作的。……类似的译作比比皆是,到后来,就是事先不知道译者,几行读下来,亦能将她给'认出来'。也就是说,张白桦在选择原作和自己的翻译文字上都在逐步形成一种独具的风格。……使她能够在不同的译作中巧用俚语,活用掌故,借用时俗。她善于用中国人最能领会的词语来表达各式各样的口吻,由此活现出不同人物的身份和此时此刻的心神和表情；她也长于用青少年最能领悟的词句来表达不同的侧面，同时展现出不同社会的氛围和当时当地的风习。"

胡晓在《中国教育报》发表的《学英语您捕捉到快乐了吗》中说："我最喜欢她的译作，因为所选篇目均为凝练精巧之作，难易适中，且多是与生活息息相关的内容，能够极大限度地接近读者。所选的文字皆为沙里淘金的名家经典，文华高远，辞采华丽。名家的经典带来的是审美的享受和精神的愉悦，含蓄隽永的语句令人不由得会心一笑；至真至纯的爱与情，轻轻拨动着人们的神经；睿智透彻的思考，让人旷达而超脱。"

综上所述，在微型小说的文化地理中，张白桦是一个独特的所在。她以独特的文化品相，承接了中华与西洋的博弈，以理论和实践造就的衍生地带，自绘版图却无人能袭。

（作者系中国作协会员，小小说作家网特约评论家，第六届小小说金麻雀提名奖获得者，本篇原载于中国作家网2015年9月9日。网址：http://www.chinawriter.com.cn）

代·序

没有微型小说汉译就没有当代微型小说

——张白桦访谈录

陈勇（中国作协会员，小小说作家网特约评论家，第六届小小说金麻雀提名奖获得者，以下简称陈）：我做微型小说评论多年，范围遍及世界华文微型小说界，您是我研究视野中出现的第一个微型小说翻译家，可能也是唯一的一个。

张白桦（以下简称张）：谢谢陈老师的青睐，我更加惊诧于您的学术识别力。因为，即使在外语界和翻译界，对于文学翻译的认识还是有许多误区的。难怪微型小说界的评论总是视译者为"局外人"，所以无人问津了。而从我的研究方向——译介学的角度来看，得出的结论是：微型小说翻译，特别是微型小说翻译文学，应该，也只是中国文学的一部分。

陈：我认同翻译与创作是国别文学的"鸟之两翼，车之两轮"之说。您能给大家普及一下文学翻译与文学创作的区别吗？

张：好的，我愿意。从文艺的本质规律来看，二者并没有分别。

从创作的内容来看，翻译的确比创作少了一道工序——构思。然而，也正是由于这一缺失，反而给翻译带来了创作所没有的困难。可以负责任地说，从创作的过程来看，正如许许多多20世纪三四十年代的作家兼翻译家共同体会到的那样，文学翻译比文学创作要难。

陈：我之所以选择了您作为评论对象，是由于您在微型小说界的独特地位和影响力，以及您在研究和实践层面全面开花的成果。

张：这倒是符合事实的。在实践方面，我在20世纪80年代初，也就是大三的时候，就翻译了第一篇微型小说，一直走下来，应该说与当代中国微型小说是共同成长的，又是唯一一个因此获奖的译者；此外，中国首部微型小说译文集"译趣坊"系列图书和中国首部微型小说自选集英译本《凌鼎年微型小说选集》也是我做的。在研究方面，是中国第一个从理论上，从宏观和微观层面，论证当代外国微型小说汉译的文学史意义的学人。

陈：您能把您的理论观点论述得详细些吗？

张：可以。当代外国微型小说汉译的翻译文学意义就在于：推动中国当代的主流文学重归文学性，重归传统诗学的"文以载道"的传统；引进并推动确立了一种新型的、活力四射的文学样式；当代微型小说汉译提高了文学的地位，直接催生并参与改写了中国当代文学史，以一种全新的文体重塑了当代主流诗学。

陈：哦，所以您才会下这样的判断："没有外国微型小说汉译，就没有当代微型小说。"是吗？

张：您的学术敏感度令人惊叹。

陈：根据我的调查统计分析，发现搞微型小说翻译实践的人虽然相对不多，却也还是有一些的。您能谈谈使您脱颖而出的"别裁之处"吗？

张：我是经历了实践—理论—再实践这样一个非线性的过程，它带给我的是对文学翻译本质的思考，对翻译艺术掌控力的把握，对文学翻译的全面观照。据我所知，微型小说译者的文化背景比较复杂，创作态度也良莠不齐。老一辈翻译家在语言文化基础和创作态度上是无可厚非的，基本表现为"全译"，可惜在文字上与原文"靠得太近"，人数也太少；中青年译者的数量居多，但语言文化基础大多不如前辈，在对原文的处理上"尺度过大"，多数表现为"编译"。

我生性保守，为人为文拘谨，记得曾经在《世界华文微型小说作家微自传》中这样总结过："回首往事，也算是'张三中'吧：'心中'的原文，'眼中'的译文，'意中'的师生。"换句话说，对原文的敬畏，对译文的时代化，对青年、妇女儿童读者的念念不忘，千方百计地贴近时代，可能因此造就我的译文忠实性和可读性较强，基本表现为"全译"。

陈：果然如此。在您的译作中，我发现有几个题材是您情有独钟的，比如，青年、妇女和儿童。也就是说，这是您自觉的文学追求，是您的"主观倾向"吧？

张：您一语中的。是的，身为女性，我"含泪的微笑"更多地落在了相似群体身上,是希望通过译作擦亮人文关怀的"镜与灯"。

陈:如果让您用几个关键词来概括您的翻译风格的话,您会选择哪些词?

张:首先进入我脑海的是:简洁、幽默、时尚。

陈:为什么是这三个词,而不是其他?

张:这个嘛,都源于我的"本色演出"。我这人简单直接,译文也就长不了;身为教书匠,我喜欢寓教于乐,译文也就搞文字狂欢;我的目标读者是青年,我的译文就各种"潮","一大波流行词语正在靠近"。

陈:嗯嗯,听出来啦。最后,我还是要不客气地指出您在创作趋势上的一个问题:您的微型小说翻译在初期量大质优,"凡有井水处,皆能歌柳词",而近期在数量上却大不如前了,希望您可以有所弥补。

张:谢谢陈老师指教,我也意识到了这个问题。原因是多方面的,最重要的还是我目前的长篇著译、教学和研究生辅导让我分身乏术。不过,我一定竭尽心力,在理论上继续为微型小说翻译"鼓与呼",在实践上做"颜色不一样的烟火"。

(本篇原载于中国作家网 2015 年 9 月 9 日。网址:http://www.chinawriter.com.cn)

目 录

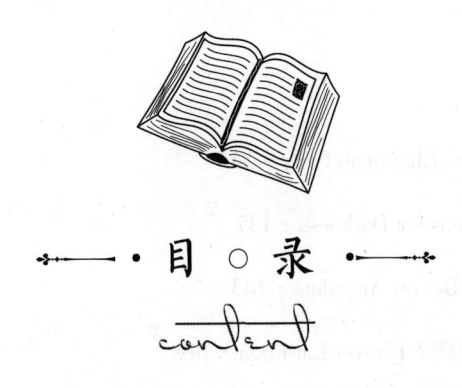

content

小写字母案 / The Case of the Lower Case Letter · 1

猫人 / The Cat Man · 7

阴差阳错 / In the Wrong Place at the Wrong Time · 17

终极武器 / The Ultimate Weapon · 38

"你是机器人吗?" / "Are You a Robot?" · 45

太空迷路 / Lost in Space · 51

通往地狱的路 / The Road through Hell · 72

哈里欧姆老年中心 / Hari Om Senior Center · 79

夺命来电 / Death Calls · 88

失落的记忆 / Forgotten Memories · 93

脑洞大开的实验 / A Most Ambitious Experiment · 108

密封的门 / The Sealed Door · 120

莫名其妙的伏击 / A Baffled Ambuscade · 126

化装舞会 / The Chanukah Party · 133

黑暗之屋 / House of Darkness · 137

河狸传奇 / A Beaver Anecdote · 143

我从来不吃比萨 / I Never Eat Pizza · 149

炸弹惊魂 / Bomb Scare · 156

一堆旧垃圾 / A Load of Old Rubbish · 163

返璞归真 / Going Back to Our Roots · 168

代价 / The Price · 177

轮到你了，轮到你了 / It's Your Turn, It's Your Turn · 186

机器人巴克斯特 / Baxter · 200

星光 / Star Light · 207

译后记 · 219

小写字母案

[美国] 杰克·德拉尼

九月的一个寒冷的早晨,她轻盈地走进我的办公室。我正一边享受着一杯上好的星巴克热咖啡,一边在网上浏览着当地新闻。著名词汇语义学教授埃德加·内特尔顿被发现死亡,头部中枪。警察判定是自杀。

她款步走过来,优雅地向我伸出一只手。我瞥见她手指上戴着一枚婚戒,上面镶嵌的宝石有巧克力豆大小。

她说:"我是伊迪丝·内特尔顿。"

"我为老先生的事感到很难过。"

"我倒没有。他爱我,但他更爱文字。长话短说,我丈夫正在写一篇论文,这篇论文将撼动词汇语义学的根基。如果把它拿来做巡回演讲,会值一大笔钱,但现在没人能找到论文了。我相信他的遗书可以提供一些线索。"

她从上衣口袋里掏出一张纸片:

伊迪丝,我不会抱怨,我的生活很好。作为一名教师,一个出售知识的人,我已经找到了财富和幸福。但是,我发现自己沮丧、绝望得无以复加……所以，我选择以自己的时间和方式死亡。我一直对你不好。我要求你把棕色的鬈发染成金发。在我应该赢得你的爱的时候，我却想我可以用钱买到你。我称你为女巫。我曾抱怨，跟我结婚的女人今何在？我说你吃得太多了。事实上，如果我想改变，我应该使用的是萝卜，而不是大棒。你可能都想要扭断我的脖子。原谅我吧。永别了。

"这封信里用的都是小写字母。但是我丈夫一直坚持使用正确的语法。我坚信这里面一定是别有用心。"

"内特尔顿太太，我想我可以帮助你。这封信有几个奇怪的地方。首先，就像你说的，全文用小写字母书写。内特尔顿先生是一位世界闻名的词汇语义学家，写信不会像少年给自己的密友一样。"

"其次，信里的同音词很多，这些词的发音相同，拼写和意思却不同。对于一个词汇语义学家来说，这肯定不是偶然的。"

"如果我们按照顺序阅读这些同音词的话，就会发现有'抱怨''卖家''小时''方式'（whine, seller, hour, manner）。按同音词转化过来的话就是：我们的庄园酒窖（Wine cellar our manor）。"

几个小时后，我们来到内特尔顿夫妇的乡间别墅，随即直奔地下室。开灯后，我们发现地窖里摆满了一排排的深色酒瓶。

"在哪里？把这个地方搜个遍可能需要好几年。"

"别着急，内特尔顿太太。首先，我要问你一件事，你婚戒上的钻石有多大？"

"8克拉。埃德加不住嘴地絮叨这事儿。"

"这就是我所担心的。"我拔出我那忠实可靠的左轮手枪。"你对他和他的词汇语义学是有什么仇、什么恨？你预谋杀了他，一人独吞论文的钱。你以为知道论文在哪里后,就强迫他写遗书。但事实上他早已对你存有戒心,于是把论文藏了起来。他给你留下了另外一个惊喜:遗书的剩余部分,没有显示论文藏在哪里,而是揭示了杀他的凶手。遗书后半部分中的同音词连起来就是:'染色、买、赢得、女巫、哪儿、吃、胡萝卜、扭断'(dyed, buy, won, witch, wheres, ate, carrot, wring)。那就是:死于一个戴8克拉戒指的人(died by one which wears eight carat ring)。"

把内特尔顿太太交给警察后,我迅速浏览了一下这个地窖迷宫。不久,我就找到了论文稿件。货架上的大部分葡萄酒都是没有包装的,但一个角落里却有两箱酒上下叠放着。我小心翼翼地打开了下面那一箱。①

---

① 原文 lower 是一个多义词,既有"小写",也有"下面"之意。——译者注

The Case of the Lower Case Letter

By Jack Delany

She breezed into my office one cold September morning. I'd been enjoying a hot cup of Starbuck's finest and surfing the web for local news. The famous lexical semanticist Professor Edgar Nettleston had been found dead, a gunshot wound to the head. The police verdict was suicide.

She held out an elegant hand as she floated towards me and I glimpsed a wedding band with a stone the size of a peanut M&M.

"I'm Edith Nettleston."

"Sorry about the old man."

"I'm not. He loved me, but he loved words more. I'll be brief. My husband was working on a paper that will rock the very foundation of lexical semantics. It's worth a fortune in lecture tours, but nobody can find it. I believe his suicide note is a clue to its whereabouts."

She removed a scrap of paper from her blouse.

"edith. i'm not going to whine, i've had a good life. i've

found wealth and happiness as a teacher, a seller of knowledge. but i find myself depressed beyond hope...and so i'm choosing the hour and manner of my own demise. i have treated you badly. i demanded you dyed your brown curls blonde. i thought i could buy you when i should have won your love. i called you a witch. i'd complain: where's the woman i married? i said you ate too much. if i wanted change, i could have used a carrot rather than a stick. you probably wanted to wring my neck. forgive me. farewell."

"It's all written in lower case. My husband was a stickler for correct grammar. I refuse to believe it doesn't mean something."

"Mrs. Nettleston, I think I can help you. There's a couple of odd things about this letter. Firstly, as you say, it's written entirely in lower case. Mr. Nettleston was a world-renowned lexical semanticist, not a teenager texting his BFFs."

"Secondly, it has a more than usual number of homophones, words where there is another word with the same sound but different spelling and meaning. When dealing with a lexical semanticist, that's surely no accident."

"If we read those homophones in order, we have: whine, seller, hour, manner. And translating to their homophones: Wine cellar our manor."

Several hours later, we arrived at the Nettlestons' country house and immediately headed for the basement. A flip of a light switch revealed tunnels filled with rows of dark bottles.

"Where is it? It would take years to search this place."

"Not so fast, Mrs. Nettleston. First I have to ask you something: your wedding ring diamond, how large is it?"

"It's eight carats. Edgar wouldn't stop talking about it."

"That's what I feared." I pulled out my trusty revolver. "How you must have hated him and his lexical semantics! You figured you'd kill him and keep the money from the paper yourself. You forced him to write that suicide note, thinking you knew where it was. But he was suspicious and he'd already hidden it. And he had another surprise for you: the rest of the note, it doesn't reveal where the paper is, it reveals his killer. The final homophones: dyed, buy, won, witch, wheres, ate, carrot, wring. That is: died by one which wears eight carat ring."

As the cops left with Mrs. Nettleston I took a quick trip round the maze of tunnels. It didn't take me long to find it. Most of the wine lay unpacked on racks but in one corner two cases sat stacked, one on top of each other. Carefully, I opened the lower one.

猫 人

[美国]罗杰·迪安·基瑟

我喜欢钓鱼。

据我所知,没有什么是比在高高的山上呼吸新鲜、清凉的空气更让人放松的事情了。我最喜欢的钓鱼地点是在一个小加油站附近的湖边,那个地方位于加利福尼亚山区的一个城镇中,从我当时住的地方出发需要三个小时的路程。

每年,冬雪刚刚融化,我便把渔具装上旅行车,出去钓一天的鳟鱼。

在一次旅行期间,我穿过形成美丽的人造高山湖泊的小水坝,把车开到一侧,开始卸下鱼竿。忽然,我听到一声枪响,子弹呼啸着飞过我的头顶。听到有人开枪射击打猎,让我大吃一惊,因为这是禁猎区,不允许打猎。另外,在我多年钓鱼的区域内,除了几辆拉木材的卡车路过,还是第一次遇到有人来。

我在汽车后面俯下身来,小心地瞭望四周,看是否有人。又响了两枪。子弹"嗖"的一声呼啸而过,击中大岩石,我却还是没有看到人。

随后,四个年轻人从土路上走来。一个人举起步枪,开了一枪。

一只猫跑过土路，钻进灌木丛。

"嗨，你们到底在干什么？"他们向我走来，我问他们。"这里禁止打猎。"

"只是打一只该死的猫。"大一些的男孩说。另一个男孩慢慢举起枪，朝着那只猫又开了一枪，猫还藏在大石块后面。

"算了吧，伙计们。干吗没来由地要杀生呢？"我问。

"依你看，那只猫值多少钱？"其中一个男孩说。

"10美元怎么样？"我说。

"砰！"他朝着猫所在的方向又是一枪。"100美元怎么样？这个价钱可以接受。"四个男孩中最大的一个说。他朝着猫所在的方向又开了一枪。

几个星期来，我一直在攒钱，想买一艘旧船和发动机，这样就可以不在岸上钓鱼了。我的钱包里有110美元，口袋里有大约20美元。

"好吧，我给你们100美元买那只猫。只是求你们不要杀死它。"我掏出钱包，从秘密夹层拿出100美元，放在棕色旅行车的引擎盖上。四个年轻人走了过来，站在那里盯着钱看。他们的脸上显出非常严肃的表情。大一些的小青年俯身拿起钱来，揣进了他的牛仔裤口袋。

四个男孩消失在土路的拐弯处，我开始寻找那只猫。

几分钟后，男孩们乘坐一辆旧的敞篷小货车从我身边驶过，回山上的镇子。

用了一个多小时，我才给了那只猫足够的信任，抓到了它。我爱抚了它5分钟左右，随后将它放进我的车里，连带我的渔具，开车回到山上的小店。

我问店主，他知不知道周围有人丢了一只猫。他走到我的车旁，看了看那只猫。他告诉我，住在隔壁的老人大约一星期前丢了自家的猫。老人很伤心,因为那是他妻子的猫,他妻子在几个星期前去世了,那只猫是她留下的全部纪念。

小店店主到电话机旁打了一个电话。他回来时,给我倒了一杯热咖啡,我们聊了大约10分钟。我听到身后的门开了,便转过身。

一位白发苍苍的老人,弯腰驼背,看上去至少有一百岁了,他慢慢地走到拐角处。在一张摇椅上坐了下来,却没有说一句话。

"那是他的猫。"店主告诉我。

老人用手杖敲了三下地板。店主从柜台后面出来,走到老人坐着的地方。老人跟店主耳语了几句,随后递给他一张纸。店主扶着老人的手臂,帮他站了起来,他们走向外面的旅行车。

我透过窗户看到老人伸手进去拿起那只猫,抱在胸前。随后,两个人走到隔壁的一栋活动住房,走了进去。

几分钟后,店主回来了。

"我真该上路了。"我告诉他。

"找到那只猫有酬谢。"店主说。

"我不要酬谢。"我回答。

可是,那个人拿出一张纸,我从他手里接过来。我打开折叠的纸,看到那是一张私人支票,可以兑换成"现金",上面写着2500美元!

我吃惊地扬起眉毛。"别担心,那张支票无效。从他妻子去世后,这位老人的神经就不正常了。"店主说。

我把支票对折后扔到柜台上,好让他扔掉。然后,我心里却有个念头,觉得应该把支票留下。于是,我把支票拿回来,放到衬衣口袋里。

"我想,只有傻瓜才认为一只猫值那么多钱。"他说着,哈哈大笑起来,声音很大。

"是呀,我知道。只有傻瓜才这么想。"我说着,也哈哈大笑起来。

我走出门,钻进旅行车,开车回家。男孩和他们的枪让我决定推迟钓鱼旅行,另找时间了。

等我到家时,妻子给了我一张便签,是一位来访的朋友留下的。便签上说他认识一个人,愿意把他的船卖给我,可按月付款。我给那位卖船的人打电话。交换完船的情况以后,我问他想要多少钱。

"2500美元。要是我替你筹措资金,就是3000美元。"他告诉我。我对他说,过一个小时后再给他打电话,给他答复。

我从口袋里拿出支票,给我存款的银行打电话。我告诉他们猫的故事,问他们是否有办法查出老人给我的支票是否有效。我把支票的号码报给他们,等着他们回话。10分钟后,电话打回来了。

"基瑟先生,支票有效。"那头的女士说着,哈哈大笑。

"有什么好笑的?"我问她。

"哦,我给银行打电话,询问这张支票是不是真的,那位先生哈哈大笑。他告诉我,那位给你支票的老人特别富有。加利福尼亚地区运营的大部分木材公司都是他的。"

无独有偶,惊喜成双。那天晚上,我驱车去看待售的船、发动机和拖车。揭开帆布时,那条船像新的一样。这笔买卖很划算,我心里明白自己想要它。但是,我看到船的名字以后,我当时就觉得这是冥冥之中注定的。

船的后面漆着的字是:猫人。

The Cat Man

By Roger Dean Kiser

I love to fish.

There is nothing that I have ever known that is more relaxing than being high up in the mountains and breathing in that fresh, cool air. My favourite fishing spot is a lake near a little one-gas-station town located high in the mountains of California—three hours from where I used to live.

Every year, as soon as the winter snow melted, I loaded my fishing gear into the station wagon and headed out for a day of trout fishing.

During one of my trips, I crossed the small dam that had been built to create the beautiful mountain lake, pulled over to the side and began to unload my fishing poles. Suddenly, I heard a gunshot ring out, whistling as it flew over my head. I was quite surprised to hear someone shooting a firearm because this was a restricted area, and no hunting was allowed. Besides, in all my years fishing the area, it was the very first time that I had ever come across anyone, except a few logging trucks passing by.

I ducked down behind my automobile and I carefully looked around to see if I could see anyone. Another two shots were fired. "Zing!" rang the bullets as they hit against the large boulders. Still, I could see no one.

Then four young men came walking down the dirt road. One raised his rifle and fired off a shot. A cat ran across the road and into the bushes.

"Hey! What the heck are you doing?" I asked them, as they approached me. "This is not a hunting area."

"Just shooting at a darn cat," said the larger boy. Slowly, another one of the boys raised his rifle and fired another shot at the cat, who was still hidden behind the large rock.

"Come on, guys. Why kill something for no reason?" I asked.

"What's the cat worth to you?" asked one of the boys.

"How about ten dollars?" I said.

"Bam!" Another shot in the cat's direction. "How about a hundred dollars? That's what it's going to take," said the largest of the four boys, as he took another shot in the cat's direction.

For weeks, I had been saving money so that I could buy some type of used boat and motor so that I would not have to fish from the bank. I had about one hundred and ten dollars in my wallet and about twenty dollars in my pocket.

"Okay, I'll give you a hundred dollars for the cat. Just don't kill it. Please." I pulled out my wallet, took the money out of the secret compartment and laid it on the hood of the brown station wagon. The four boys walked up and stood looking at the money. A very serious look came over their faces. The older boy reached down and picked up the money and put it into his jean pocket.

As the four boys disappeared around the bend of the road, I began to look for the cat.

Several minutes later, the boys, in an old pickup truck, drove past me, headed back up the mountain towards town.

It took me over an hour to get the cat to trust me enough so that I could catch it. I petted her for five minutes or so and then I put her into my vehicle, along with my fishing gear and drove back up the mountain to the little store.

I asked the owner if he knew if anyone in the area had lost a cat. He walked out to my vehicle and looked at the cat. He told me that the old man who lived next door had lost his cat about a week ago. The old man was very upset because it was his wife's cat and she had died several months before and the cat was all that he had left.

The owner of the small store went to the telephone and made a call. When he returned, he poured us a hot cup of coffee and we talked for about ten minutes. I heard the door open behind me and I turned around.

A grey-haired man, all hunched over, who looked to be at least

100 years old, slowly made his way to the corner. He sat down in a rocking chair, but didn't say a word.

"It's his cat," the owner told me.

The old man tapped his walking cane three times on the floor. The owner came from behind the counter and walked over to where the old man was sitting. The old man whispered something to the owner and then handed him a piece of paper. The owner took the old man by the arm, helped him up, and they walked outside to the station wagon.

I watched through the window as the old man reached in and picking up the cat, hugged it to his chest. Then the two men walked to a mobile home next door and went inside.

Several minutes later, the store owner came back.

"I had best be hitting the road," I told him.

"There's a reward for finding the cat," the store owner said.

"I don't want a reward," I replied.

But the man held out a piece of paper and I took it from him. I opened the folded paper and saw that it was a personal cheque made out to "CASH" and written in the amount of $2500!

I raised my eyebrows in surprise. "Don't worry, that cheque is no good. The old man has been off his rocker since his wife died," said the store owner.

I folded the cheque in half and I threw it onto the counter so that he could throw it away. Then something inside me told me to keep the cheque. I picked it back up and placed it into my shirt pocket.

"I guess only an idiot would think that a cat is worth paying that kind of money for," he said, as he laughed out loud.

"Yeah, I know. Only an idiot would think like that," I said, laughing too.

I walked out the door, got into my station wagon and I drove home. The boys and their guns had made me decide to postpone my fishing trip until another time.

When I arrived home, my wife handed me a note a friend of mine had dropped by. The note said he knew a man who would sell me his boat on a monthly payment plan. I telephoned the man with the boat. After discussing the boat, I asked him how much he wanted for it.

"$2500. Or $3000 if I have to finance it for you," he told me. I told him that I would telephone him back in about an hour.

Taking the cheque out of my pocket, I telephoned my bank. I told them the story and I asked them if there was any way to find out if the cheque that the old man had given me was any good. I gave them the numbers off the cheque and I waited for them to call me back. Ten minutes later the call came in.

"Mr. Kiser, the cheque is good," said the woman, laughing.

"What's so funny?" I asked her.

"Well, when I called the bank to ask if the cheque would clear, the gentleman there laughed. He told me that the old man who gave you the cheque is extremely wealthy. He owns most of the logging companies that operate in that area of California."

And that wasn't the only surprise. That evening I drove over to see the boat, motor and trailer that were for sale. When the tarp was removed, the boat was like new. It was a great deal. I knew I wanted it. But when I saw the name of the boat, I decided right there that it was meant to be.

Painted on the back of the boat were the words: The Cat Man.

阴差阳错

[美国] 比尔·普洛奇尼

有时候事情就是这样,毫无征兆,无法防备。但这不是你的错,你只不过是在错误的时间出现在了错误的地点。

夜里 11 点,细雨蒙蒙,云层低垂,能见度很低。我在弗雷斯诺连续办了四天案子,现在正归心似箭地回旧金山的家。开车沿着 99 号公路往西穿过几座丘陵和山谷就能到达 152 号公路,它是连接 99 号公路和 101 号公路之间最快的捷径。路边的加油站和便利店挂着灯牌,牌子上写着"营业到午夜 12 点"。一辆老式车停在洗手间外的阴影里,这时一辆崭新的别克车开进了加油站。便利店的玻璃连同上面的广告牌已被雨水打湿,店里有人,但人影模糊不清。

我不需要加油,但的确需要喝杯热咖啡提提神,也想吃点东西来填饱饥肠辘辘的肚子,离开弗雷斯诺的时候时间不够,没来得及吃一口东西。我一个急转弯拐进加油站,把车停在了那辆老式车旁。下车打了个哈欠,我伸了伸懒腰,经过别克车走向便利店,长驱直入。

还没看到带枪的小个子家伙的时候,我就感觉有问题。气氛有问题——沉闷、欲爆裂般,像暴风雨来之前的气氛。顿时,我感觉后脑勺的头发竖了起来,但是已经迈进了门,走了两步,退出已经来不及了。

那个小个子家伙紧挨着薯片架站着,两手握枪贴在胸前。另外两名男子站在10英尺开外的柜台处,两人一个在柜台前,一个在柜台后。那把手枪——一把长枪筒的打靶手枪,正对着柜台前的一个人。小个子的头向我所在的方向侧了侧,但手里枪的方向没变。此时,我停下了脚步一动不动,双臂下垂紧贴身体两侧。

时间像是被冻结了似的。我们四个人互相凝视,大家都一动不动。小雨敲打着屋顶,发出的声音像某种机器发出的微弱的喘鸣声——除此之外,再没有其他声音。

拿枪的小个子突然咳了一声,这声像得了肺痨的人才有的干咳打破了沉默,却加剧了紧张气氛。他身材瘦小干枯,35岁左右的样子,秃顶,脸圆鼓鼓、紧绷绷的,两只棕色的眼睛距离很近,眼里有深仇大恨,有怒不可遏。柜台后的店员20来岁,长发扎成了马尾,他不停地舔着嘴唇,使劲儿咽着唾沫,双眼快速环视着四周,一会儿定睛凝视,一会儿一闪而过,定睛凝视时,双眼像一对紧张的苍蝇。他已经吓得魂飞魄散,但仍竭力自控。柜台前那个40来岁的帅哥却完全不一样。他的眼睛就没离开过手枪,仿佛枪对他有什么催眠作用似的。汗水让他那毫无血色的脸颊变得光滑,一滴滴小小的汗珠从下巴滚下。他的恐惧一目了然,病态、粗鄙,全神贯注;你能看到恐惧在他的汗珠下、皮肤下爬行,就像蛆在腐肉块里蠕动。

"哈里,"他的声音谄媚且畏缩,"哈里,看在上帝的分儿上……"

"闭嘴,不要叫我哈里!"

"听着……不是我,是诺琳……"

"闭嘴!闭嘴!闭嘴!"声音尖利、刺耳且嘶哑。"你,"他对我说,"到这儿来,我好看着你。"

我靠近柜台,动作很慢。这不是我起初所设想的持枪抢劫——小个子和帅哥之间有点私事，几分钟前它在这里演变成了这场致命的危机。和我一样，年轻的店员也是在错误的时间来到了错误的地点。

我说："究竟怎么回事？"

"我要杀死这个狗娘养的，"小个子说，"就是这么回事。"

"你为什么要杀他？"

"我的妻子、我的积蓄，我在这个世界赚到的每一分钱……都被他夺走了，现在他得为此付出代价！"

"哈里，求求你，你要——"

"不是叫你闭嘴嘛！不是告诉你不要叫我哈里嘛！"

帅哥摇了摇头，一种毫无意义的胡乱摆动，像白色竿子上破碎的电灯泡。

"她在哪儿，巴洛？"小个子质问道。

"诺琳吗？"

"我的婊子老婆诺琳。她在哪儿？"

"我不知道啊……"

"她不在你那儿。你出门时屋子里黑着。诺琳不会一个人待在黑房子里的。她怕黑。"

"你——看到我在屋里了？"

"对。我看见你了，还跟踪你20英里才到了这儿。你难道以为我会突然神秘地出现吗？"

"你盯我的梢？趴窗户？天哪——"

"我到的时候你正要出门，"小个子说，"完美的时机。你难道没想过我会查出你的名字和住处吗？你以为你很安全，是不是？愚蠢的老哈里·查尔方特，戴着绿帽子呢，傻子——没的怕的。"

帅哥的头又摇了摇，这次摇落了几粒汗珠。

"但我还是查出来了。"小个子说。"我花了整整两个月的时间,终于找到你了,现在我要杀了你。"

"别这么说,你不会,你不能……"

"继续,求我啊,求我不要杀你。"

巴洛呻吟着,身子向后用力靠着柜台。致命的恐惧会让一些人变得愁闷,他像我见过的其他人一样也变得意志消沉。没过多久,他开始跪在地上乞求起来。

"诺琳在哪儿?"

"我发誓,我真不知道,哈里——查尔方特先生,她……几天前……抛弃了我,卷走了所有的钱。"

"你的意思是我的一万美元还剩了一些?我还以为都挥霍空了呢。不过没关系,我已经不在乎钱了,我只在乎让你付出代价。你,然后诺琳。你俩都得付出代价,你们罪有应得。"

查尔方特渴望让他们付出代价,好吧,是渴望要他们的命。但是希望和事实是两码事。子弹上了膛,一切准备就绪。他也进入了一个过度情绪化的状态,但他不是一个真正的杀手。这种情况下你可以通过观察一个人的眼睛——我已经观察过很多次了,辨别这个人是否能成为一名冷血杀手。冷血杀手的眼里有一团火,闪烁着死亡之光,他们目标明确,不可改变,而在哈里·查尔方特的眼睛里是看不到这些的。

但没有这样的眼神并不意味着他就不危险。此时的他兴奋异常、怒不可遏、仇恨满腔,近乎白色的手指扣在扳机上。任何时候一个不经意的动作都可能射出一颗子弹,甚至两颗。一旦走火,子弹会落在任何地方——击中巴洛,或年轻的店员,或者我。

小个子说:"她是我的一切。我的工作、积蓄、生命……没有遇见她以前,这些对我毫无意义。矮小、丑陋、孤独……这就是我。但她曾经爱过我,至少爱过我一点,足以让她嫁给我。然后你来了,你毁了这一切!"

"我没有!我告诉你,这一切都是她的主意……"

"闭嘴!都是你,巴洛,你让她变了心,你把她带坏了。你这个该死的旅行推销员,你这该死的陈词滥调。你一定还有其他女人。你为什么就不能离她远点儿!"

他越发激动了,这足以刺激他扣下扳机。我想过突袭,但发现这并不是个好主意,因为我们之间的距离太远,他随时可能开枪。还有另一种选择,只能孤注一掷了。

我心平气和地说:"把枪给我吧,查尔方特先生。"

话音落下,他并没有反应,我又重复了一遍。这次他眨了眨眼,虽然头没有动,但视线移向了我。"你说什么?"

"把枪给我。结束这一切,以免为时过晚。"

"不可能,闭嘴。"

"你不想杀任何人。你知道的,我也知道。"

"他要付出代价。他们都得付出代价。"

"好吧,让他们付出代价。按盗窃罪起诉他们,把他们送进监狱。"

"这太便宜他们了。"

"你不同意,那是因为你没有尝过蹲大狱的滋味。"

"你尝过蹲大狱的滋味吗?你是什么人?"

半真半假比实话实说、和盘托出更有力。"我是一名司法人员。"我回答道。

巴洛和店员都猛地转过头看着我。年轻的店员眼中充满了希望,但帅哥没有,他的恐惧还在发酵,没有减弱。

"你撒谎。"查尔方特说。

"我为什么要撒谎?"

他又咳嗽了一声,痰液卡在了喉咙深处。"这没什么区别,你阻止不了我。"

"是,我阻止不了你射死巴洛。但我可以阻止你杀死你的妻子。我已经下班了,但枪还在身上呢。"这是深思熟虑后说的谎言。"如果你杀了他,那我必须杀你。你的枪一响,我就开枪,你也得死。你可不希望这样。"

"我不在乎。"

"你在乎,是的,从你脸上就能看出来。查尔方特先生,你不想今晚死于非命。"

这倒是真的:他不想,也看不到他的身上有死亡之光。

"我必须让他们付出代价。"他说。

"你已经让巴洛付出了代价。你看看他现在的样子——他在付出代价呢。为什么要杀死他让他脱离苦海呢?"

有那么一会儿,查尔方特石柱一般僵立在那儿,枪已收到了胸前。他伸出舌头,保持着这样的姿态像猫一样,这让他看起来像斗鸡眼。第一次,他变得不确定起来。

"你不想死,"我又说了一遍,"承认吧,你不想死。"

"我不想死。"他承认了。

"你不想店员或者我死,对吗?如果你开枪,我们很可能就会死。你的手里就会沾上无辜人的血。"

"是的。"他说,"的确,我不希望那样。"

我已经向前慢慢地小心翼翼地迈了两步,又试着迈了一大步。枪口仍对准巴洛的胸口。我看了看查尔方特的食指,他似乎放松了对扳机的控制,双手也不再那么紧握着武器。

"让我拿着枪吧，查尔方特先生。"

他没有说话，也没有动弹。

我张开双手，慢慢、慢慢地靠近了一步。

"把枪给我。你不想死在今晚，没有人要死在今晚。把枪给我吧。"

我又向前迈出一步。突然，就像石板瞬间被擦亮，所有的怒不可遏、满腔仇恨、复仇的欲望都从他眼里消失了。他没有看我，只用一只手把枪从胸前挪开，递给我。我轻轻接过枪，将其放进上衣口袋。

就这样，危险解除。

店员如释重负，突然大声吐出一口气，近乎虔诚地说道："噢，天哪！"巴洛瘫软地靠着柜台，呜咽着，随后骂了查尔方特几句脏话。他过于沉浸在自己和刚才的脱险上了，反而没有对小个子表示太多的恨意。他也没看我。

我抓住查尔方特的手臂，领他绕到柜台后面，让他坐在那里的一张小凳子上。他现在目光呆滞，舌头又从唇间伸了出来，显得温顺驯服，无所适从，心灰意冷。

"快报警。"我对店员说。"当地的、县里的都行，哪儿最快就打哪儿。"

"县里。"说着他一把抓起了电话。

"让他们带一个医护小组来。"

"是，长官。"然后他说，"嘿！嘿！那家伙要走了。"

我立刻转身，发现巴洛已经溜到门口，门眼看就要关上了。我冲年轻的店员大喊一声，让他看好查尔方特，然后我便拔腿去追巴洛。

他钻进了停在加油泵旁边的别克车里，门砰地关上了，我没等他锁上门，就快步上前猛地拉开门。"你哪儿也不许去，巴洛。"

"你没有权利把我扣在这儿——"

"谁说没有!"

我迅速低头侧身进了车里,他企图跟我搏斗。我用一个胳膊肘把他挤在座位上,并伸出另一只手从点火装置上拔下了车钥匙。这时他不再挣扎,我于是放开他退了出去。

"下车!"

他吊儿郎当、摇摇晃晃地下了车,靠在敞开的车门上看着我,眼里写满了恐惧。

"为什么急着离开?为什么这么怕我?"

"我没怕你……"

"你肯定是怕我,就像你怕查尔方特和他的枪一样,也许更怕我。我说我是警察的时候你的脸上都露出来;直到现在,你还很恐惧呢。你汗流浃背像头猪似的,为什么?"

他又软塌塌地摇了摇头,跟我还是没有眼神接触。

"你今晚为什么到这儿来?来这样一个特别的地方?"

"我要加油……"

"查尔方特说他跟了你20英里。肯定有比这家离你家更近的加油站开放。半夜三更的还下着雨——你为什么舍近求远?"

他又摇了摇头。

"一定是上路后才意识到快没油了吧。"我说,"也许你心不在焉了,心里想着别的事。比如今晚家里发生的事,一些你怕查尔方特偷偷摸摸扒着窗户查你时看见的事儿。"

我打开别克车的后门。座椅上和车厢里都是空的。然后我绕到车尾,把他的一把钥匙插进后备厢的锁孔里。

"不!"巴洛跌跌撞撞地走到车后,一把抓住我,企图把我推开。我用肩膀把他挤到一边,转动钥匙,打开了后备厢。

后备厢塞着一具裹在塑料薄膜里的尸体。

一只惨白的手臂露在外面,手指弯曲成钩状。我扯开塑料薄膜的一头,刚好能大致看到那张死去的女人脸。皮肤上有斑点,舌头发黑,伸了出来。一看就是因窒息而死。

"诺琳·查尔方特。"我问他,"你要把她带到哪里,巴洛?带到偏远的深山上埋了?"

他失声恸哭,发出像野兽受伤的声音。"噢,上帝啊,我不是故意要杀死她的……我们因为钱的事吵了一架,我失去了理智,我不知道自己在做什么……我不是故意要杀她的……"

他的腿支撑不住了,于是他一屁股坐到了人行道上,两腿张开,头垂了下来,然后就再也没有动弹过,只有胸膛在上下起伏。他的脸湿得更厉害了,汗水、雨水,还有泪水混在一起。

我朝蒙着水汽的橱窗望去。我想,那个可怜的混蛋还在那儿。他想让他的妻子为她的所作所为付出代价,但发现巴洛已经替他完成这一切的时候,他的精神会崩溃的。

我关上后备厢,冒着严寒站着,等待着警察的到来。

有时候事情就是这样。

你在错误的时间来到了错误的地点,但事情仍然能如人所愿。反正,对某些涉案人员来说是这样的。

In the Wrong Place at the Wrong Time

By Bill Pronzini

Sometimes it happens like this. No warning, no way to guard against it. And through no fault of your own. You're just in the wrong place at the wrong time.

Eleven p.m., drizzly, low ceiling and poor visibility. On my way back from four long days on a case in Fresno and eager to get home to San Francisco. Highway 152, the quickest route from 99 west through hills and valleys to 101. Roadside service station and convenience store, a lighted sign that said "Open Until Midnight." Older model car parked in the shadows alongside the restrooms, newish Buick drawn in at the gas pumps. People visible inside the store, indistinct images behind damp-streaked and sign-plastered glass.

I didn't need gas, but I did need some hot coffee to keep me awake. And something to fill the hollow under my breastbone: I hadn't taken the time to eat anything before leaving Fresno. So I swung off into the lot, parked next to the older car. Yawned and stretched and walked past the Buick to the store. Walked right into it.

Even before I saw the little guy with the gun, I knew something was wrong. It was in the air, a heaviness, a crackling quality, like the atmosphere before a big storm. The hair crawled on the back of my scalp. But I was two paces inside by then and it was too late to back out.

He was standing next to a rack of potato chips, holding the weapon in close to his body with both hands. The other two men stood ten feet away at the counter, one in front and one behind. The gun, along-barreled target pistol, was centered on the man in front; it stayed that way even though the little guy's head was half turned in my direction. I stopped and stayed still, with my arms down tight against my sides.

Time freeze. The four of us staring, nobody moving. Light rain on the roof, some kind of machine making thin wheezing noises—no other sound.

The one with the gun coughed suddenly, a dry, consumptive hacking that broke the silence but added to the tension. He was thin and runty, mid-thirties, going bald on top, his face drawn to a drum tautness. Close-set brown eyes burned with outrage and hatred. The clerk behind the counter, twenty-something, long hair tied in a ponytail, kept licking his lips and swallowing hard; his eyes flicked here and there, settled, flicked, settled like a pair of nervous flies. Scared, but in control of himself. The handsome, fortyish man in front was a different story. He couldn't take his eyes off the pistol, as if it had a hypnotic effect on him. Sweat slicked his bloodless face, rolled down off his chin in little drops. His fear was a tangible thing, sick and rank and consuming; you could see it moving under the sweat, under the skin, the way maggots move inside a slab of bad meat.

"Harry," he said in a voice that crawled and cringed. "Harry, for God's sake..."

"Shut up. Don't call me Harry."

"Listen...it wasn't me, it was Noreen..."

"Shut up shut up shut up." High-pitched, with a brittle, cracking edge. "You," he said to me. "Come over here where I can see you better."

I went closer to the counter, doing it slow. This wasn't what I'd first taken it to be. Not a hold-up—something personal between the little guy and the handsome one, something that had come to a lethal crisis point in here only a short time ago. Wrong place, wrong time for the young clerk, too.

I said, "What's this all about?"

"I'm going to kill this son of a bitch," the little guy said, "that's what it's all about."

"Why do you want to do that?"

"My wife and my savings, every cent I had in the world...he

took them both away from me and now he's going to pay for it."

"Harry, please, you've got to—"

"Didn't I tell you to shut up? Didn't I tell you not to call me Harry?"

Handsome shook his head, a meaningless flopping like a broken bulb on a white stalk.

"Where is she, Barlow?" the little guy demanded.

"Noreen?"

"My bitch wife Noreen. Where is she?"

"I don't know..."

"She's not at your place. The house was dark when you left. Noreen wouldn't sit in a dark house alone. She doesn't like the dark."

"You...saw me at the house?"

"That's right. I saw you and I followed you twenty miles to this place. Did you think I just materialized out of thin air?"

"Spying on me? Looking through windows? Jesus..."

"I got there just as you were leaving," the little guy said. "Perfect timing. You didn't think I'd find out your name or where you lived, did you? You thought you were safe, didn't you? Stupid old Harry Chalfont, the cuckold, the sucker—no threat at all."

Another head flop. This one made beads of sweat fly off.

"But I did find out," the little guy said. "Took me two months, but I found you and now I'm going to kill you."

"Stop saying that! You won't, you can't..."

"Go ahead, beg. Beg me not to do it."

Barlow moaned and leaned back hard against the counter. Mortal terror unmans some people; he was as crippled by it as anybody I'd ever seen. Before long he would beg, down on his knees.

"Where's Noreen?"

"I swear I don't know, Harry...Mr. Chalfont. She...walked out on me...a few days ago. Took all the money with her."

"You mean there's still some of the ten thousand left? I figured it'd all be gone by now. But it doesn't matter. I don't care about the money anymore. All I care about is paying you back. You and then Noreen. Both of you getting just what you deserve."

Chalfont ached to pay them back, all right, yearned to see them dead. But wishing something and making it happen are two different things. He had the pistol cocked and ready and he'd worked himself into an overheated emotional state, but he wasn't really a killer. You can look into a man's eyes in a situation like this, as I had too many times, and tell whether or not he's capable of cold-blooded murder. There's a fire, a kind of death light, unmistakable and immutable, in the eyes of those who can, and it wasn't there in Harry Chalfont's eyes.

Not that its absence made him any less dangerous. He was wired to the max, and outraged and filled with hate, and his finger was close to white on the pistol's trigger. Reflex could jerk off a round, even two, at any time. And if that happened, the slugs could go anywhere—into Barlow, into the young clerk, into me.

"She was all I ever had," he said. "My job, my savings, my life...none of it meant anything until I met her. Little, ugly, lonely... that's all I was. But she loved me once, at least a little. Enough to marry me. And then you came along and destroyed it all."

"I didn't, I tell you, it was all her idea..."

"Shut up. It was you, Barlow, you turned her head, you corrupted her. Goddamn traveling salesman, goddamn cliche. You must've had other women. Why couldn't you leave her alone?"

Working himself up even more. Nerving himself to pull that trigger. I thought about jumping him, but that wasn't much of an option. Too much distance between us, too much risk of the pistol going off anyway. One other option. And I'd damn well better make it work.

I said quietly, evenly, "Give me the gun, Mr. Chalfont."

The words didn't register until I repeated them. Then he blinked, shifted his gaze to me without moving his head. "What did you say?"

"Give me the gun. Put an end to this before it's too late."

"No. Shut up."

"You don't want to kill anybody. You know it and I know

it."

"He's going to pay. They're both going to pay."

"Fine, make them pay. Press theft charges against them. Send them to prison."

"That's not enough punishment for what they did."

"If you don't think so, then you've never seen the inside of a prison."

"What do you know about it? Who are you?"

A half-truth was more forceful than the whole truth. I said, "I'm a law officer."

Barlow and the clerk both jerked looks at me. The kid's had hope in it, but not Handsome's; his fear remained unchecked, undiluted.

"You're lying," Chalfont said.

"Why would I lie?"

He coughed again, hawked deep in his throat. "It doesn't make any difference. You can't stop me."

"That's right, I can't stop you from shooting Barlow. But I can stop you from shooting your wife. I'm off duty but I'm still armed." Calculated lie. "If you kill him, then I'll have to kill you. The instant your gun goes off, out comes mine and you're also a dead man. You don't want that."

"I don't care."

"You care, all right. I can see it your face. You don't want to die tonight, Mr. Chalfont."

That was right: He didn't. The death light wasn't there for himself, either.

"I have to make them pay," he said.

"You've already made Barlow pay. Just look at him—he's paying right now. Why put him out of his misery?"

For a little time Chalfont stood rigid, the pistol drawn in tight under his breastbone. Then his tongue poked out between his lips and stayed there, the way a cat's will. It made him look cross-eyed, and for the first time, uncertain.

"You don't want to die," I said again. "Admit it. You don't want to die."

"I don't want to die," he said.

"And you don't want the clerk or me to die, right? That could happen if shooting starts. Innocent blood on your hands."

"No," he said. "No, I don't want that."

I'd already taken two slow, careful steps toward him; I tried another, longer one. The pistol's muzzle stayed centered on Barlow's chest. I watched Chalfont's index finger. It seemed to have relaxed on the trigger. His two-handed grip on the weapon appeared looser, too.

"Let me have the gun, Mr. Chalfont."

He didn't say anything, didn't move.

Another step, slow, slow, with my hand extended.

"Give me the gun. You don't want to die tonight, nobody has to die tonight. Let me have the gun."

One more step. And all at once the outrage, the hate, the lust for revenge went out of his eyes, like a slate wiped suddenly clean, and he brought the pistol away from his chest one-handed and held it out without looking at me. I took it gently, dropped it into my coat pocket.

Situation diffused. Just like that.

The clerk let out an explosive breath, said, "Oh, man!" almost reverently. Barlow slumped against the counter, whimpered, and then called Chalfont a couple of obscene names. But he was too wrapped up in himself and his relief to work up much anger at the little guy. He wouldn't look at me either.

I took Chalfont's arm, steered him around behind the counter and sat him down on a stool back there. He wore a glazed look now, and his tongue was back out between his lips. Docile, disoriented. Broken.

"Call the law," I said to the clerk. "Local or county, whichever'll get here the quickest."

"County," he said. He picked up the phone.

"Tell them to bring a paramedic unit with them."

"Yes sir." Then he said, "Hey! Hey, that other guy's leaving."

I swung around. Barlow had slipped over to the door; it was just closing behind him. I snapped at the kid to watch Chalfont and ran outside after Barlow.

He was getting into the Buick parked at the gas pumps. He slammed the door, but I got there fast enough to yank it open before he could lock it. "You're not going anywhere, Barlow."

"You can't keep me here—"

"The hell I can't."

I ducked my head and leaned inside. He tried to fight me. I jammed him back against the seat with my forearm, reached over with the other hand and pulled the keys out of the ignition. No more struggle then. I released him, backed clear.

"Get out of the car."

He came out in loose, shaky segments. Leaned against the open door, looking at me with fear-soaked eyes.

"Why the hurry to leave? Why so afraid of me?"

"I'm not afraid of you..."

"Sure you are. As much as you were of Chalfont and his gun. Maybe more. It was in your face when I said I was a cop; it's there now. And you're still sweating like a pig. Why?"

That floppy headshake again. He still wasn't making eye contact.

"Why'd you come here tonight? This particular place?"

"I needed gas..."

"Chalfont said he followed you for twenty miles. There must be an open service station closer to your house than this one. Late at night, rainy— why drive this far?"

Headshake.

"Has to be you didn't realize you were almost out of gas until you got on the road," I said. "Too distracted, maybe. Other things on your mind. Like something that happened tonight at your house, something you were afraid Chalfont might have seen if he'd been spying through windows."

I opened the Buick's back door. Seat and floor were both empty. Around to the rear, then, where I slid one of his keys into the trunk lock.

"No!" Barlow came stumbling back there, pawed at me, tried to push me away. I shouldered him aside instead, got the key turned and the trunk lid up.

The body stuffed inside was wrapped in a plastic sheet.

One pale arm lay exposed, the fingers bent and hooked. I pulled some of the sheet away, just enough for a brief look at the dead woman's face. Mottled, the tongue protruding and blackened. Strangled.

"Noreen Chalfont," I said. "Where were you taking her, Barlow? Some remote spot in the mountains for burial?"

He made a keening, hurt-animal sound. "Oh God, I didn't mean to kill her...we had an argument about the money and I lost my head, I didn't know what I was doing...I didn't mean to kill her..."

His legs quit supporting him; he sat down hard on the pavement with legs splayed out and head down. He didn't move after that, except for the heaving of his chest. His face was wetter than ever, a mingling now of sweat and drizzle and tears.

I looked over at the misted store window. That poor bastard in there, I thought. He wanted to make his wife pay for what she did, but he'll go to pieces when he finds out Barlow did the job for him.

I closed the trunk lid and stood there in the cold, waiting for the law.

Sometimes it happens like this, too.

You're in the wrong place at the wrong time, and still things work out all right. For some of the people involved, anyway.

终极武器

[爱尔兰] 索尔·格林布拉特

物理学家、工程师卡尔·多布森博士和西莉亚·摩尔博士被带到一个秘密军事基地,做一个特殊的项目。当他们抵达时,受到了凯斯将军的接见,凯斯将军是基地的指挥官。"欢迎你们,多布森博士和摩尔博士,很高兴见到你们。"他边说边与他们握手。凯斯带他们参观了基地的设施以后,把他们带到了实验室。"我相信,你们会发现你们的实验室是与众不同的。"他说着,他们走进了实验室。

"伙计,这是实验室。"西莉亚说。

"当然。"卡尔环顾四周。

"坐下吧,我来告诉你们国家想让你们做什么。我们的科学家一直在从理论上说明,让一个物体消失是可能做到的。如果可能的话……你可以想象一下。经过长时间的寻找,我们决定由你们两位专家来做这件事,假如可以做到的话。"

"将军,我读过所有已经出版的科学杂志,但是我从来没有见过与这个理论相关的任何论文。在某种程度上,我希望我已经有了方案。这个方案非常有趣。给我和西莉亚一个月的时间,如果一个月结束的时候我们提不出什么办法,我们会告诉你的。"卡尔说。

第二天早上，卡尔和西莉亚来到他们的实验室，讨论了情况。"卡尔，你真的在考虑这种可能性吗？"

"是的，西莉亚。我几乎彻夜未眠，听我说。我的理论是，一股强大的力量，无论是光或声音，都需要使原子向分子不断的运动停止。问题是当一个物体中不断运动的原子和分子停止运动时会发生什么？那时我睡着了。"

"因此，能够使分子停止运动的力量是一种什么力量？极端的低温或高温？还是两者都不是？如果原子和分子停止运动，我们如何知晓？如果它们停止运动的话，该物体会发生什么？物体会破碎吗？物体会融化吗？"西莉亚不解。什么能产生脉冲力？

"就这样，将产生脉冲力的机器画在绘图板上。"

"接下来的一周他们会设计一系列具有内部机制的技术装置，当这些装置被激活时，就会产生脉冲。最新的设备靠电池驱动，外形像一个老式的大口径短枪，从枪管中发出脉冲，得让他们相信这是值得测试的。我们用什么东西作为测试目标呢？"卡尔说。

"金属垃圾桶怎么样？"

"好的，西莉亚。把桶放在工作台上，我去拿枪。"他把枪扛在肩上，西莉亚走到15英尺开外。卡尔端起枪，退后大约10英尺，瞄准了目标，发射。这股力量把卡尔打得站不起来，把篮子打到了房间的另一头。西莉亚急忙把他扶了起来。

"卡尔，我们知道这个设想是正确的。看一下垃圾桶。"她说着，检查了一下。"哎哟，太烫了，还损坏了。"

"是的。我认为我们上了正确的轨道。我们需要更大的力量。"

"我也是这么想的，卡尔。有一件事很清楚，它必须安装远程发射。"

"电子发电机太小了,还有……西莉亚,如果我们把发电机的能量和重复脉冲激光结合起来,你认为会产生什么效果?我们可以修改激光器以增加功率输出。告诉凯斯将军我们需要什么。"他说着给将军打了电话,将军急忙赶到了实验室。他们告诉他,他们需要什么、在哪儿能找到,他在五天内都给送到了实验室。

卡尔和西莉亚对枪进行了改装。"好吧,西莉亚,我们来试试。"

"卡尔,我觉得我们不应该在屋里测验。我们制造了一个功能强大的设备,但我们不知道它会造成什么损害。这位将军想要一种能让敌人消失的武器,我们不知道我们的设备是否具有这种能力。"

"你说的对。我们和凯斯将军说,用他不介意消失的东西建一个靶场。"

第二天,在离武器60英尺远的地方安放置了一辆卡车,武器放置在一堵10英尺高的墙外,墙里有一扇窗户。凯斯将军和他的工作人员在他的办公室里观看。

"好吧,西莉亚,我有一种感觉,我们已经研发出了终极武器。过一会儿,那辆卡车就会消失。"他说着把触发装置递给了她。"你来尽地主之谊。"

"谢谢,我可以,但我有点担心。我不知道我们制成的是什么装置,不知道这种武器有什么效果,这让我很紧张,但我们必须测试,所以开始吧。"她说着,按下了遥控器上的"点火"按钮。

离武器20英里远的科顿布拉夫小镇,一股烟雾有节奏地从小镇上空飘过,继续向前移动,小镇正在分崩离析。最终,烟雾掩盖了整个星球以及地球上的一切;建筑物、武器、人类、森林都消失了。这颗星球的表面变成了尘埃。人们不再需要终极武器,因为已经没有能战斗的军队了。

The Ultimate Weapon

By Saul Greenblatt

Dr. Carl Dobson, a physicist and engineer, and Dr. Celia Moore were brought to a secret military facility to work on a special project. When they arrived they were met by General Case, the commander of the facility. "Welcome Dr. Dobson, Dr. Moore, I'm pleased to meet you," he said and shook their hands. After showing them around the facility, Case took them to their lab. "I'm sure you'll find your lab exceptional," he said and they entered the lab.

"Boy, this is some lab," Celia said.

"It sure is," Carl said looking around.

"Let's sit down, and I'll tell you what your country wants from you. Our scientists have been theorizing that it might be possible to make an object disappear. If it were possible…well, you can imagine. After a lengthy search, it was decided that you two are the experts who could do it if it can be done."

"General, I've read every scientific journal that is published and I have never seen anything about this theory. In a way, I wish I had thought it up. It is intriguing. Give me and Celia a month. If at the end of the month, we can't come up with something, we'll tell you." Carl said.

The next morning, Carl and Celia went to their lab and discussed the situation. "Carl, are you actually entertaining the possibility that it can be done?"

"Yes, Celia. I thought about it most of the night. Hear me out. I theorize that a powerful force, light or sound, would be needed to stop constantly moving atoms and molecules from moving. The question is what would happen to an object when its constantly moving atoms and molecules stopped moving? That's when I fell asleep."

"So, what kind of force would stop molecules from moving? Extreme cold, heat? Neither? And how would we know if the atoms and molecules stopped moving, and if they did stop, what would happen to the object? Would the object come apart? Would the object melt?" Celia posed. What could generate a force a pulse?

"That's it. A machine that generates pulses of energy. To the drawing board."

"For the next week, they designed a variety of technical devices with internal mechanisms that, when activated, generated pulses. The latest device, which was battery operated, was shaped like a blunderbuss, emitted pulses out of the barrel, and led them to believe it was worth testing. What shall we use as a target?" Carl said.

"How about the metal waste basket?"

"Okay, Celia. Put the basket on the work counter and I'll get the gun ready." He rested the gun on his shoulder, and Celia moved about fifteen feet away. Carl stepped back about ten feet, aimed, and shot the weapon. The force knocked Carl off his feet, and blew the basket across the room. Celia rushed to help him up.

"Well, Carl, we know the concept is valid. Let's look at the waste basket," she said and the examined it. "Ouch, it's hot, and it's mangled."

"Yeah. I think we're on the right track. We need more power."

"I think so, Carl, and one fact is clear. It has to be mounted and fired remotely."

"The electronic generator is too small, and…Celia, what do you think would happen if we combined the energy from the generator with a repetitively pulsed laser? We could modify the laser to increase the power output. Let's tell General Case what we need," he said and phoned the General who hurried to the lab, and they told him what they needed and where to get the items, which he delivered to the lab in five days.

Carl and Celia made the changes and additions to the gun. "Well, Celia, let's try it out."

"Carl, I don't think we should test this inside. We've built a powerful device and we don't know what damage it can do. The General wants a weapon that will make the enemy disappear, and we don't know if we have it."

"You're right. Let's tell General Case to set up a firing range with something he won't mind seeing disappear."

The next day, a truck was placed twenty yards from the weapon, which was outside a ten-foot-high wall with a window in it. General Case and his staff watched from his office.

"Well, Celia, I have a feeling that we have the ultimate weapon. In a little while, that truck will disappear," he said and handed her the triggering device. "You do the honors."

"Thanks. I don't mind, but I'm a little apprehensive. I don't know what we have created, and not knowing what the weapon can do makes me nervous, but we have to test it, so here goes," she said, and pressed the "fire" button on the remote.

The small town of Cotton Bluff, twenty miles from the weapon, disintegrated as a cloud of pulsating vapor passed over the town and moved on. Eventually, it covered the planet, and everything; buildings, weapons, people, forests disappeared. The planet's surface was reduced to dust. There was no longer a need for the ultimate weapon, for there were no armies left to fight.

"你是机器人吗？"

[英国] 格雷丝·鲁思

公园长凳上方的水果树硕果累累，风在树枝间呼啸而过，吹得苹果像芭蕾舞演员一样摇摇摆摆。头上的天空一望无际，蔚蓝、清澈、万里无云，但对约翰·史密斯来说，这似乎不是个阳光灿烂的日子。

约翰坐在绿色公园的长凳上，旁边是蜿蜒穿过公园向后延伸的小径。他闭着眼睛，头向后仰，树在脸上投下了忽明忽暗的光影。一位女士戴着耳塞，推着婴儿车在慢跑，没有注意到这个坐在椅子上的高个儿男人。这个男人高兴地坐在那里看着，或者更准确点说，是听着，就好像世界在围着他转。

"先生？你好？"约翰睁开眼睛，刺眼的阳光让他直眨眼。

"你好？"他回答道，然后用手揉了揉眼皮。他可能睡着了，也可能没有，很难说。

一个小女孩站在他旁边，头上的金发梳成了马尾辫，一双绿色的眼睛。一条牛仔工装裤的带子垂在她瘦小的胳膊上。她指着他的腿，问道："先生，你是机器人吗？"

约翰顺着她的手往下看。他的两条不一样的腿暴露在阳光下，其中一条腿是正常的，棉质袜子盖过脚踝，红色的匡威鞋在草地上打着简单的节拍。另一条腿是黑色金属和塑料，本来是一条腿，但是现在变成了假肢。他明白她为什么觉得他是个机器人。他心不在焉地揉着腿，脸上露出严肃的笑容。在他看来，这原本就不是个阳光灿烂的日子，而现在却觉得灰蒙蒙的，要有暴风雨。

"哦，你是问这个吗？"他问。女孩点点头。他告诉她，"很久以前，我……我在一场战争中失去了一条腿。"他的声音有点哽咽。约翰在心里对自己摇了摇头。那是很久以前的事了。当想到这个事情的时候，他握紧了拳头，又松开垂在身体的两侧，红色的匡威鞋继续在地上打着简单的节拍。"你看我像机器人吗？"

女孩抬头用大大的眼睛看着他，但约翰没有再注意她。当他不看自己的腿的时候，他几乎可以忘记战争，忘记发生在他身上的一切……医生说他这是创伤反应，情绪会反复无常，会内心迷惘。

"嗯，机器人就是机器。"女孩说。约翰把手放进大衣的口袋里。外面越来越凉了。不知怎么的，感觉没有那么暖和了。

"你是一台机器，约翰，不是吗？杀人的机……"

约翰把手从口袋里掏出来，手里握着一把微型手枪。然后这支枪发出了消音手枪的消音声，伴着红色的飞溅和一声短促的喊声，小女孩的头向后仰去。周围没有人听见，也没有人关心。医生们说他情绪会反复无常，看来他们说的是对的。

约翰又把枪放回夹克口袋里，把头从孩子那边转过来，盯着远处，视线越过那棵硕果累累的苹果树。

"干得好，混蛋，你找到我了。"

小女孩的头不自然地立了起来。约翰是一名神枪手，子弹射向哪儿完全由他决定。她的头倒在了肩膀上，像齿轮一样咔嗒作响，把自己重新装配在了一起。一只大眼睛仍是绿色的，另一只眼睛则是个黑色的、烧焦的洞，透过她的头艰难地凝视着他。

"约翰，我们一定会找到你的。"女孩的头往一侧倾斜了一下，然后又倾斜到另一侧。此刻她的脸隐在苹果树的阴影里，她残忍地笑了笑。她的眼睛反射在约翰的眼镜上，也反射在他的眼睛里。"你无处遁形了。"

"Are You a Robot?"

By Grace Ruth

The wind sighed through the fruit-laden branches that hung over the park bench, sending the apples swaying like dancers in a ballet. The sky stretched overhead, blue and clear and cloudless, but for John Smith, it didn't seem a sunny day.

John sat on the green park bench by the side of the paved walking trail that wound through the park, leaning against the back. His eyes were closed and his head tilted back, the patterns of light and dark cast by the tree twisting across his face. A lady jogged by with earbuds and a stroller, oblivious to the tall man on the bench. He was happy there to sit and watch, or rather, listen, to the world spin around him.

"Mister? Hello?" John opened his eyes, blinking as the sunlight hit them.

"Hello?" He asked, rubbing a hand across his eyelids. He might've fallen asleep, he might not have. It was hard to tell.

A little girl with blonde pigtails and wide, green eyes was

standing beside him. One strap of her stained jean overalls was falling down her skinny arm. She pointed at his legs. "Are you a robot, Mister?"

John looked down along with her. His mismatched legs were stretched out in the sunlight. One was normal, cotton sock stretching above his ankle and red converse tapping a simple beat on the grass. The other was black metal and plastic, a prosthetic where his leg used to be. He could see why she thought of him as a robot. He rubbed his leg absently, his face dropping into a stern grin. It hadn't seemed like a sunny day to him before, but now it felt grey and stormy.

"Oh, this?" He asked. The girl nodded. "I-I lost my leg in a war a long time ago." He told her, his voice catching a bit. John shook his head at himself mentally. It had been ages ago. His hand curled into a fist as he remembered and he dropped it back to his side. The red converse foot continued the simple beat. "Do I look like a robot to you?"

The girl looked up at him with big eyes, but John wasn't paying attention to her anymore. When he wasn't looking at it, he could almost forget the war, forget everything that had happened to him...The doctors all called him traumatized, unstable, confused.

"Well, robots are machines." The girl was saying. John tucked his hands inside his coat's pockets. It was getting chilly outside. Somehow, the sun didn't feel quite so warm.

"And you're a machine, John, aren't you? A killing ma-"

John's arm snapped out of his pocket, a tiny pistol in his fist. There was the muffled noise of a silenced gun and the little girl's head snapped backwards with a splash of red and a bit of a cry. There wasn't anyone around to hear, or care. They told him he was unstable. They were right.

John tucked the gun away inside his jacket again, turning his head away from the child and staring into the distance, past the knotted trunk of the apple tree.

"Well done, bastards. You found me."

The little girl's head moved upwards unnaturally. John had the aim of an expert marksman. The bullet went where he wanted it. Her head settled back on her shoulders with a clacking like gears fitting themselves back together. One eye was still wide and green. The other was a black, charred hole staring strait through her head.

"We will always find you, John." The girl's head tilted one way, then back the other. Her face was caught in the shadows of the apple tree now, and she smiled brutally. Her eyes were reflected in John's glasses, in his very eyes. "There's no where you can hide."

太空迷路

[美国] 罗兰·马修·克里斯滕森

"集合!"马吉先生在楼下客厅一声高喊,房子的四面八方都爆发出"啪嗒啪嗒"的响声。女孩有莱利、利什、哈莉、多尼和艾丽卡,从她们皇家规模般的房间冲下楼来。她们在那里用枕头、毛巾和亚麻布建造了一座堡垒,马吉太太曾特别叮嘱她们不要用亚麻布。

房子的对面,有一连串的门猛地被打开,又冲出几个孩子。男孩有弗莱彻、哈德逊、雷,还有这群孩子里最小的一对双胞胎古拉和威尔,全都涌出各自的房间,在楼梯顶撞到一处。

就像训练有素的足球队,每个人都各就各位。根据个头大小排列,古拉和威尔站在前面,女孩们站在双胞胎和其他男孩之间。

"我们要去国家航空航天博物馆。"马吉先生宣布。"每个人都将进入'超级堡垒'。"

所谓的"超级堡垒",其实就是家里的面包车,用"二战"时的B-29重型轰炸机命名,叫"超级堡垒"。这辆面包车是辆有15个座位的庞然大物。只有借助"超级堡垒",才能运送规模如同小型部队的这一家人。大家都按照惯例各就各位,古拉和威尔在车的右后角系好了安全带。

"你要是不赶紧放下那台平板电脑,手就会被慢慢吸进屏幕,你会变成一个电子人。"古拉对威尔冷嘲热讽着。威尔正在平板电脑上玩银河帝国星际战机。过了一会儿,古拉继续说:"不过想想,要是有个电子人兄弟,那就太棒了!继续玩吧。"

双胞胎之一的古拉精力充沛,体格健壮。他的真名叫巴顿,以"二战"中一位著名的将军命名(马吉先生热衷于二战史),大家却都叫他古拉,把他看作童话《黑海的古拉》中那个顽皮的小怪兽。对他来说,这个名字很合适。

威尔选择对哥哥的讽刺言论不予理会,他全神贯注地玩着银河帝国星际战机。在威尔的心目中,电子游戏不仅仅是打发时间的消遣,其中还包含了一个完整的故事。电子游戏需要具备解决问题的能力,需要创造力,还需要手眼协调。古拉最大的爱好是足球,也许玩游戏的手眼协调不能与之相比,但对威尔来说,这是一个值得花时间的爱好。

"超级堡垒"挤进一个停车位,"轰隆"一声停下来。马吉太太说:"好啦,伙计们,你们都知道规矩。别走散,待在一起,绝对不要在博物馆里追逐打闹。"马吉先生跟着说:"把你的平板电脑放在车里,威尔。"古拉正准备插话,马吉先生又冷嘲热讽了一句,打断了他:"也不能带足球,古拉。"

马吉一家人大踏步地走向博物馆的入口处,两扇巨大的自动滑门打开了,将他们一家人引向博物馆的大厅。马吉先生和太太给大家买了票,带着孩子们穿过旋转门,进入第一展厅:美国宇航局的太空探索。这个大型展览包括各种探测器、太空舱、无人驾驶飞机和宇宙飞船。这个展览折射了美国太空计划取得的巨大成就,对古拉和威尔来说,却是趣味无穷的游乐场。

古拉轻推了一下威尔,指着房间远处一架形状奇特的飞机。"威尔，看那架飞机！看起来就像'超级堡垒'。我们应该问问爸爸妈妈，他们会不会给家里买下来。我们去看看吧！"

"那不是普通飞机，是航天飞机！"威尔边跑边喊，追上已经冲向航天飞机的孪生兄弟。

"太大了！"古拉叫道。威尔赶上他，注意到在进入航天飞机的门口处拉着黄色带子。门上挂的牌子写着"禁止入内"。古拉很快理解为，这个牌子只是说不准从这里进入，可以找别的入口。

"有个舱口！"古拉躲在航天飞机伸出的机翼下，在飞机腹部下方发现了一个小入口。

"古拉，别打开。咱们要是跟家人走散，爸爸妈妈永远都不会让咱们有出头之日了。"古拉犹豫了一下，思考着双胞胎兄弟刚才所说的后果。他从舱口退回来，不过只是暂时克制着。

古拉把嘴角鼓成圆形，对着威尔露出恶魔式的假笑。"你做什么鬼脸？"威尔不解地问。

"我要打开舱门进去。你要是离开我，我就会跟家人走散。你回到爸爸妈妈那里时，他们会问你是否知道我在哪里，你必须解释为什么要把我一个人留下。"

"不行。古拉，我要回去找家人……我们要回去找家人！你要是打开那个舱门，弄不好咱们会被踢出博物馆！"威尔强调。

古拉对威尔稀松平常的威胁不以为然。他根本不理睬他，径直走向那扇微型门。他把手放在舱口的操纵杆上，回头看了看威尔，做出挑衅的手势。

"别这样，古拉。"威尔恳求道。

"你是要和我一起去探索这艘宇宙飞船，还是想回去玩银河帝国太空战机？"

"这是星际战机。对,我宁愿回去玩我的游戏。"

听到这话,古拉毫不犹豫地伸出手,抓住操纵杆,向下转了九十度。舱口打开,冒出一股灰尘。

"我们进去。"古拉笑着说。

不等威尔说出更多他们不应进入太空船的理由,古拉就进到舱内,转动把手,按下按钮,打开舱室。"威尔,银河帝国太空战机有这样的宇宙飞船吗?"

威尔溜过舱门说:"那是星际战机。没有,银河帝国只有外星飞船,这是一艘人类的飞船。"

"你得承认,这太棒了!对不对?"古拉夸口道。

威尔正要回答,只听身后传来"咔嗒"一声响。是舱门的动静,门突然关上了。威尔急忙到门口,拉动里面的操纵杆。操纵杆一动不动,不愿回到原位,依旧停留在古拉进来时扳到的90度位置。

"锁上了!"威尔抱怨道。

"我们该怎么办?"古拉的假笑早已不见了,换成了忧虑的表情。

"想啊,想啊!"威尔敦促道,"在银河帝国的星际战机中,有一项任务是,你必须潜入敌人的飞船,窃取他们宇宙大炮的密码。"

"这不是电子游戏,威尔,说正经的,咱们被困在里面啦!"听起来,古拉像是后悔自己当初进入航天飞机的决定。"等爸爸妈妈意识到我们走散了,我们的麻烦可就多啦。"

"某个地方肯定还有出口,到处找找看。"威尔指点着。"我没看到,但有一架梯子升到了另一层。"

"我觉得只有这个选择了。咱们试试。"

这对双胞胎爬上梯子,周围包裹着狭窄的圆柱形管子。他们到达第二层,进入了航天飞机内部一个更大的空间。这个舱里有两个带橡胶轮的金属支架。

"我们进入货舱了。"威尔说,"我们需要找到驾驶舱,很可能就在我们现在所在位置的正上方。到了那里,我们就能看到外面,发出求救信号。"

"你怎么这么了解这艘飞船?"古拉问。

"银河帝国的外星飞船的驾驶舱,就在起落架的正上方。所以,咱们就盼着这艘飞船跟那些飞船类似吧。"

在寻找出路时,这对双胞胎没有找到任何出口。

"看,"威尔指着天花板说,"那里有另一个舱门,但没有上去的梯子。"

"我没看到有梯子……可是我看到了上去的路。"古拉回答。

不等威尔问清楚,古拉就爬上了一个围着起落架的金属壳顶部。从那里,他伸手摸到了像是通风系统的边缘。他好像一只太空猴。看着孪生兄弟攀上缩小版的航天飞机的顶部,在下面观看的威尔很有把握,此时不由得笑出了声。

"你笑什么?"古拉说。他接近了舱口。

"你一路爬上去,看起来就像一只黑猩猩。你真的很擅长这个。"

"谢谢,"古拉回答,"这跟我们上周体育课参加的攀岩差不多。咱们就盼着这个舱门能通向航天飞机的驾驶舱吧。"

古拉右手握着横在太空飞船内部的一条银色管道,左手伸向舱门的操纵杆。他转动操纵杆,舱门猛地打开。古拉伸出左手把自己固定在出口,一只脚向上踢去,脚挡住了打开的舱门。只用了几秒钟,他便爬出舱门。

"嘿!"古拉叫道。"这里有个梯子,我可以放下去给你。"片刻后,梯子从舱口滑下来,伸到下面的威尔跟前。

"你说的对，"古拉承认，"驾驶舱就在拐角处。我们看看是否能给博物馆的人发个信号，救我们出去。"

机身很小。驾驶舱只有容纳两个座位的空间，两个座位配有各种各样的安全带和扣环，被当作复杂的座椅安全带。座椅前面有一个控制面板，遍布着按钮、开关和操纵杆。控制面板上的东西都在尖叫："推我，扭这个，转那个开关。"古拉立即服从指令。他按了一下面板中间的黄色大按钮，扭动上方的三个绿色开关。这是一个充满想象力的主题乐园。

"威尔，我们现在正驾驶着美国国家航空航天局的宇宙飞船！虽然我们偷偷溜进宇宙飞船遇上了麻烦，可我想不出博物馆里还会有比这更有趣的东西！"

威尔完全同意，坐下来笑着自言自语："是啊。这比银河帝国星际战机酷多了。"

古拉继续表演操纵航天飞机，拉着停在两个机长座位之间的操纵杆。"准备登上月球吧，威尔船长。"他开玩笑说。

威尔微笑起来。他仔细端详着控制面板，眼睛紧盯着一个看起来很重要的按钮。"倒计时着陆！"威尔哈哈大笑。

在一个干净的方形盒子里，有一个鲜红色的按钮，上面有一个感叹号。他伸出右手，掀开塑料外壳。"五、四……开始降落！"他欢呼着，按下按钮。

驾驶舱响起一阵轻微的吱吱声，吓坏了这对双胞胎。"你按了什么按钮？"古拉问。

"我不知道，可确实起作用了。我们去看看。"

两个男孩从座位上转出来，穿过机身向后走。威尔注意到航天飞机的舱壁透出一道光，感到很奇怪。"嘿，看，这是另一个舱口。这就是那个按钮的用途!"

"紧急出口!"古拉喊道。

古拉推开舱门,想从航天飞机里找到出路,回到博物馆的底层。他把头探出舱外,四处张望,很快又把头缩了回来。

"你想先听好消息还是坏消息?"他问威尔。他的表情似乎变得不妙。

"嗯,先听坏消息。"威尔回答。

"我们所在的位置特别高,我看不出有什么办法从这里下去。"

"那么,好消息呢?"

"好消息是,除此之外,再也没有坏消息了。"古拉半真半假地笑着说。

"我们该怎么办?"古拉问道,"你会在银河帝国飞船里做什么?"

"在星际战机!"

"对不起,银河帝国星际战机。"古拉夸张地说。

"嗯,某个地方一定有装着补给品的应急箱。我们也许能在那个箱子里找到有用的东西。"

"对啊!"古拉喊道。"我看见机长的椅背上卡着一个,就在驾驶舱里!"

他们从座位上抓起应急箱,"咔嗒"一声打开盖子。古拉在箱子里翻找,拿出一根卷起来的绳索。"这个!就是这个。我们可以把绳索系在舱门上,然后从航天飞机一侧下到地面。"古拉热情洋溢地解释道。

"你疯了!"威尔反驳道。

"听着,"古拉尽量让威尔平静下来,"我们在这里已经待得太久了。要是爸爸妈妈现在还没有注意到我们不在,他们肯定随时会发现。我们必须尽快离开这艘宇宙飞船,回到家人身边。这就是我要做的。我要用这根绳索从航天飞机滑落到地上。你要是不想和我一起去,祝你能找到另一条出路。"

古拉还没等威尔做出回应,便朝舱口走去,把绳索系在航天飞机内壁上一个结实的固定装置上,然后爬了出去。

"下面见。"

"等等!"威尔喊着,却没能阻止古拉。他从航天飞机滑了下去,只留下了一缕空气。他的脚轻轻着地,松开了绳索。威尔的头转来转去,想看看是否有人注意到他的孪生兄弟从飞船一侧滑了下去。他似乎太谨小慎微,不愿这样做。

"快点!"古拉说,抬头盯着威尔。威尔抓住绳索,觉得与其犹豫不决在恐惧的深渊中越陷越深,还不如马上离开。

他们做到了。这对双胞胎成功逃离了他们原本偷偷溜进的航天飞机。"家人在哪里?你看见他们了吗?"

"咱们最好找到这里的工作人员,告诉他们,咱们迷路了。"威尔回答。"咱们回博物馆大厅吧。"

这对双胞胎回到了博物馆的前面,经过在参观展览时看到的那些科技小发明。威尔指着一名身穿红领衬衫、胸前印有美国宇航局标志的女士说:"那个人看起来像是这里的工作人员。我去问问。"

威尔刚想张口引起工作人员的注意,古拉就抓住了他的手臂。"瞧!咱们家的人!他们正从前门走出去。他们肯定在不知道咱们失踪的情况下,看完了其他展品!咱们去追上他们吧!"

"超级堡垒"的门开了,滑过轨道,露出15个座位的汽车内部。这对双胞胎从后面跟着大家一窝蜂地冲进来,挤着从家人中间穿过。古拉和威尔爬过前两排座位,在"超级堡垒"的角落里安顿下来。除了几声哼哼,以及对他们硬是挤进面包车的抱怨声,家人对他们的失踪一无所知。

跟轰隆轰隆进车位一样,"超级堡垒"从停车位又轰隆轰隆地出了车位,慢虽然慢,却有条不紊。

"嘿,"古拉低声说,"我能和你一起玩银河帝国星际战机吗?"

威尔咧嘴一笑,把平板电脑递给了他的孪生兄弟。

Lost in Space

By Roland Mathew Christensen

"Round up!" called Mr. Magee from the downstairs living room. The house erupted with pitter patter from every direction. The girls: Riley, Lish, Hallie, Donie and Erika came rushing downstairs from their imperial sized room where they had been constructing a fortress out of pillows, towels and linen, of which Mrs. Magee specifically told them not to use the linen.

From the opposite wing of the house, a series of doors whipped open flushing out several more children. The boys: Fletcher, Hudson, Ray and the youngest of the bunch: twins, Gula and William all spilled out of their respective rooms colliding into each other at the top of the stairwell.

Everyone came sliding into position like a well-coached football team. Arranged by size, Gula and William were standing in front while the girls positioned themselves in-between the twins and the rest of the boys.

"We're headed to the National Air and Space Museum,"

declared Mr. Magee. "Everyone into the Super-Mag."

The Super-Mag was the family van. Named after the World War II B-29 Heavy Bomber, The Super-Fortress. The family van was a 15 seat monstrosity. Transporting a family the size of a small army was only doable with the help of the Super-Mag. Everyone settled into their customary seating arrangement while Gula and William buckled up in the back right corner of the van.

"If you don't let go of that iPad soon, your hands are going to slowly absorb into the screen and you'll become a Cyborg," taunted Gula directing his comment towards William who was playing Imperial Galactic Star fighters on his iPad. After a short pause Gula continued by saying, "On second thought, it would be awesome having a cyborg brother. Keep Playing."

Gula was the energetic and athletic twin. His actual name was Patton in Honor of a WWII general (Mr. Magee was a WWII fanatic) but everyone called him Gula after a playful fairy tale monster, *The Gula of the Black Sea*. It was quite a fitting name for him.

William chose not to respond to his brother's sarcastic remark. He kept his focus on Imperial Galactic Starfighters. In William's mind, video games were more than just trivial distractions to pass the time, they held an entire story within them. Video games required problem solving, creativity, and hand eye coordination. Maybe not as much hand eye coordination as Gula's favorite hobby; Football, but they were a worthwhile hobby to William.

The Super-Mag came to a rolling stop as it wedged into a parking spot. "Alright guys, you all know the drill. Stay together and absolutely no roughhousing with each other inside the museum," stated Mrs. Magee. "Leave your iPad in the car, William," trailed Mr. Magee. Right as Gula was about to chime in with yet another sarcastic remark Mr. Magee cut him off, "No footballs either, Gula."

As the Magee family strode up to the entrance of the Museum, two massive automated sliding doors opened showing the family into the lobby of the Museum. Mr. and Mrs. Magee purchased everyone's tickets and ushered their children through the revolving portals leading into the first exhibit: NASA's Space Exploration. The vast exhibition contained various rovers, capsules, drones and spacecraft. It was a looking glass into the colossal achievements of the United States Space Program but to Gula and William it was a limitless playground.

Gula nudged William, pointing to an oddly shaped aircraft in the far corner of the room. "Will, Look at that airplane! It almost looks like the Super-Mag. We should ask Mom and Dad if they'll buy it for the family. Let's go check it out!"

"That's not an airplane, it's a space shuttle!" shouted William as he ran to catch up with his twin brother who was already in full sprint towards the shuttle.

"It's humongous!" exclaimed Gula. As William caught up with his brother he noticed yellow tape strewn across the door that led into the shuttle. Hanging on the door was a sign that read "Keep Out". Gula quickly categorized the sign as only a suggestion of exclusion and was already looking for another way in.

"A hatch!" Gula ducked below the shuttle's outstretched wing where he discovered a small entryway just underneath the belly of the aircraft.

"Gula, do not open that. Mom and Dad will never let us see the light of day if we get lost from the family." Gula hesitated, thinking of the consequences his twin sibling had just stated. He backed away from the hatch, though only momentarily subdued.

The corners of Gula's mouth rounded, forming a devilish smirk that was aimed right at William. "What are you doing with your face?" questioned William, dubiously.

"I'm opening this hatch and going in. If you leave me, I'll get lost from the family. When you go back to Mom and Dad they'll ask you if you know where I am and you will have to explain why you left me alone."

"No. Gula, I am going back to find the family…WE are going back to find the family! If you open that hatch, we might even get kicked out of the museum!" asserted William.

Gula shrugged off William's lackluster of a threat. Ignoring him altogether he walked straight up to the miniature door. Putting his hand on the Hatch's lever, he looked back at William as a sign of provocation.

"Don't do it, Gula," pleaded William.

"Are you gonna come explore this spaceship with me or do you want to go back and play Imperial Galactic Spacefighters?"

"It's Starfighters and yes, I'd rather go back and play my game."

With no hesitation this time, Gula flexed his hand, gripping the lever as he twisted it ninety degrees downward. The Hatch gave way, exhaling a puff of dust as it opened.

"We're in," smiled Gula.

Before William could give more reasons as to why they should not enter the spaceship Gula was well inside, twisting knobs, pushing buttons and opening compartments. "Will, do they have spaceships like this one in Imperial Galactic Spacefighters?"

William slipped through the hatch, "It's Starfighters and no, I.G.S only has alien spacecraft. This is a human ship."

"You've got to admit, this is pretty awesome! Right?" boasted Gula.

As William was about to answer he heard a clicking noise come from behind him. It was the Hatch. It had swung shut. William hurried over to it pulling on the inside lever. It was stiff, unwilling to budge the ninety degrees Gula had turned it on the way in.

"It's locked!" groaned William.

"What do we do?" Gula's smirk was long gone. A look of concern had replaced it.

"Think. Think!" William urged, "In imperial Galactic Starfighters there's a mission where you have to sneak into the enemy's ship and steal the codes to their cosmic cannon."

"This isn't a videogame, Will. Get serious. Were trapped inside!" Gula started to sound like he was regretting his decision to enter the shuttle. "We are going to be in loads of trouble when Mom and Dad realize we're gone."

"There must be another exit somewhere. Look around," directed William. "I don't see one, but there's a ladder that goes up to the next level."

"I don't think we have a choice. Let's check it out."

The twins started up the ladder, encased by a narrow cylindrical tube. As they reached the second floor they entered an even larger cavity within the shuttle. Inside this cavity was two metal legs with rubber wheels attached.

"We're in the cargo bay," said Will. "We need to find the Flight Deck. It's probably straight above where we are right now. From there, we'll be able to see outside and signal for help."

"How do you know so much about this ship?" asked Gula.

"The alien spacecraft cockpits in I.G.S are right above their landing gear. So let's hope this ship is similar."

Searching for a way out, the twins failed to find any means of an exit.

"Look," said William pointing to the ceiling, "there's another hatch up there but no ladder leading up to it."

"I don't see a ladder...but I do see a way up," responded Gula.

Before William could ask, Gula climbed on top of a metal casing that surrounded part of the landing gear. From there he reached for the edge of what looked to be part of the ventilation system. He was a space monkey. Even William, watching safely from the ground, laughed at the sight of his twin brother scaling the inside of the shuttle.

"What are you laughing at?" Gula asked as he neared the Hatch.

"You look like a chimpanzee climbing all the way up there. You're really good at it."

"Thanks," replied Gula, "It's similar to the climbing wall we went to for Physical Education class last week. Let's just hope this Hatch leads to the shuttle's Flight Deck."

With his right hand holding onto a piece of silver piping that lined the interior of the spacecraft, Gula reached for the hatch's lever using his left hand. He twisted the lever and the hatch thrust open. Gula kicked his foot up through the open hatchway, reaching with his left hand to position himself inside the doorway. He was through the opening in mere seconds.

"Hey!" called out Gula. "There's a ladder up here that I can drop down to you." Moments later a ladder slid down through the hatchway reaching William at the bottom.

"You were right," admitted Gula. "The Flight Deck is right around the corner. Let's see if we can signal to someone in the museum to help us get out."

The fuselage was quite small. There was only enough room for two seats which were equipped with various straps and buckles that acted as complicated seat belts. Positioned in front of the seats was a control panel littered with a multitude of buttons, switches, and levers. Everything on the control panel screamed, "Push me, twist this, flip that switch." Gula immediately complied. He pushed a huge yellow button in the center of the panel, flipping three green switches just above that. It was a theme park of imagination.

"Will, we are flying a NASA spaceship right now! Even if we do get in trouble for sneaking onto a spaceship, I can't think of anything more fun to do inside a museum!"

In utter agreement, William sat back and smiled to himself. "Yea. This is much, much cooler than Imperial Galactic Starfighters."

Gula continued to act like he was steering the shuttle, pulling on the joystick which rest in between the two captain's seats. "Prepare to land on the moon, Captain Will," he joked.

William smiled. He studied the control panel, his eyes locked onto a button which looked to be of considerable significance. "Countdown to landing!" William laughed.

Housed in a clear, square casing was a bright red button with an exclamation mark pictured on it. He reached out to his right and flipped open the plastic casing. "Five, Four...Initiate landing!" he cheered, pushing the button.

A soft creaking noise stirred about the Flight Deck, startling the twins. "What button did you press?" asked Gula.

"I don't know but it did something. Let's go see."

The boys spun out of their seats and walked back through the fuselage. Curious, Will noticed a crevice of light that was gleaming through the shuttle wall. "Hey, look its another hatchway. That's what the button was for!"

"Emergency exit!" shouted Gula.

Gula pushed the hatch open, seeking a way out of the shuttle and back down to the ground floor of the museum. Popping his head outside the hatch to look around, he swiftly popped his head back inside again.

"Do you want the good news or the bad news first?" he asked Will, whose facial expression seemed to take a turn for the worse.

"Ummm, the bad news first," responded William.

"We are extraordinarily high up and I see no way of getting down from here."

"So what's the good news then?"

"The good news is, there is no more bad news," laughed Gula half-heartedly.

"What can we do?" challenged Gula. "What would you do in Imperial Galactic Space fighters?"

"It's Starfighters!"

"Sorry, Imperial Galactic STAR fighters," Gula exaggerated.

"Well there must be an emergency kit somewhere with supplies. We may be able to find something useful in that kit."

"Yea!" exclaimed Gula. "I saw one stuck to the back of the captain's chair, inside the Flight Deck!"

They grabbed the kit off of the seat and clicked its lid open. Rummaging through the box, Gula pulled out a curled up rope. "This! This is it. We can tie off the rope to the hatchway and rappel down the side of the shuttle to the ground," explained Gula, enthusiastically.

"Are you crazy!" retorted William.

"Listen," said Gula trying to calm his brother down, "we've been in here for a long time. If Mom and Dad haven't noticed we're gone by now, they are sure to notice any minute. We've got to get out of this spaceship and back to the family as fast as possible. So here's what I'm gonna do; I'm gonna use this rope to slide down the shuttle to the ground. If you don't want to come with me, good luck finding another way out."

Gula didn't wait for his brothers response. He walked towards the hatchway, knotted the rope around a sturdy fixture attached to the inside wall of the shuttle and climbed out.

"See you at the bottom."

"Wait!" yelled William. It was no use. Gula was descending down the shuttle leaving behind nothing but a wisp of air. His feet touched down softly, letting go of the rope. William's head was swiveling back and forth, looking to see if anyone had noticed his twin brother rappelling down the side of the spacecraft. He seemed overly cautious to do the same.

"Come on!" mouthed Gula, staring up at William. William grabbed hold of the rope and decided it was better to go forthwith than to hesitate and allow fear to plunge any deeper.

They had done it. The twins successfully escaped from the shuttle they had originally snuck into. "Where's the family? Do you see them?"

"We better find someone who works here and tell them we are lost," William replied. "Let's go back to the museum lobby."

The twins made their way back to the front of the museum, passing the same gizmos and gadgets they saw on their way into the exhibit. Pointing towards a woman wearing a red collared shirt with the NASA logo on the front, "That person looks like they work here. I'll ask them," said William.

Just as William was opening his mouth to catch the attention of the staff member, Gula grabbed his arm. "Look! The family! They're walking out the front doors. They must have gone through the rest of the exhibits without even knowing we were missing! Let's catch up to them!"

The doors of the Super-Mag opened, gliding down it's tracks to expose the inside of the fifteen seater. The twins came barreling in from behind, bulldozing their way through the rest of the family. Climbing over the first two rows of seats, Gula and William settled into their corner of the Super-Mag. With the exception of a few groans and complaints about their rugged entry into the van, the family was oblivious to their disappearance.

The Super-Mag rolled out of it's parking space the same way it rolled in, slow and methodically.

"Hey," whispered Gula, "can I play Imperial Galactic Starfighters with you?"

William grinned and handed his iPad to his twin brother.

通往地狱的路

[澳大利亚] 大卫·凯恩斯

"慢点!"

"为什么?"皮特问道,稍稍松了下油门。"现在是凌晨三点钟。警察都睡了。把那瓶酒给我!"

"这太危险了。"他的女友凯利回答道。她已经痛苦了很长时间了,然后不情愿地把瓶子递给了他。她已经习惯了他超速行驶的嗜好和无视安全的犯罪行为。以大声辱骂的方式发出的紧急提醒,通常是能使他保持清醒的手段,但这维持不了多长时间。

"天太黑了。"她说。

"现在是晚上,笨蛋!"他们总是在晚上兜风。事实上,他们每件事都是在晚上做的。她不知道为什么,但他们就是这样。在一片令人窒息的黑暗中过着偶尔兴奋的生活。这条狭窄的公路的左边出现了一个标志,在车灯刺眼的光线下闪烁着。凯利用一种假装有兴趣的语调大声地读了出来,就像往常一样,嘲笑黛博拉·温格在《忘记巴黎》里的老父亲。

欢迎来到地狱。

新南威尔士一个整洁的小镇。

653号

"想在地狱过夜吗，亲爱的？""你为什么不直接开进天堂去呢？"凯利说，她想让自己听起来像在开玩笑。她从来没有感觉这么害怕过，而且这不仅仅是因为这个小镇的名字。还因为一个影子走到前面的路上，在他们面前晃了几秒钟，然后就消失了。这是她想象出来的吗？它回来了，就像被一台无形的压气机充了气似的迅速变大，并开始形成一个不规则的球体。那是什么东西？皮特能看到吗？

她指了指，但是皮特已经看到了，慌张地想看得更清楚些。"见鬼，那是什么？"他关掉了远光灯，然后又打开，看看这是不是光的问题。并不是。这个形状变得更大了，很快又有另一个加入，然后又来了一个。皮特惊慌失措地握住方向盘，他那两只缺乏血色的双手散发着幽灵般的光芒，照在他的脸上，但他并没有放慢速度。"是动物吗？我看不见。我看不出来！"

凯利被吓呆了，当她看到第三个形状从道路下面渗出时，那可怕的恐怖面具令人窒息。这三个东西保持着速度，一直在车前面，然后突然合并成一个，新的无形实体比汽车还大。

当他们惊恐地盯着它时，一个巨大的畸形脑袋从黑色无形团的中心伸了出来，紧接着是两只胳膊，然后是两条长而有力的腿。它在跑！它转过身来看着他们，带着一个大大的微笑，没有牙，两个布满血丝的眼球漂浮在撕裂的肉海中，调皮地看着前方。凯利顿时尖叫起来。

皮特抓狂了，疯狂的恐惧感令他不由自主地加大油门，因为那个可怕的幽灵把整个庞大的身躯转到了他们面前。它倒转过来，嘲笑他们。"我要杀了你，滚开，我要杀了你！"皮特咆哮着。"我要杀了你，滚开,我要杀了你!"野兽般令人不安的、低沉而刺耳的声音在车内放大了。

就在这只奔跑的生物举起手掌,在路中间死死地停下来的那一瞬间,汽车撞到了一棵树上,一分为二。扭曲的金属和塑料像一文不值的垃圾一样,在寒夜的冷空气中四分五裂,还裹着人体的残骸。第二天早上,这对年轻夫妇遗体的残骸在路标旁被发现,就像站在草地里的哨兵。跪着的医生站起身来,向警官点头示意,警官用毯子盖住了那个女人的脸。他看了看告示牌,伤心地摇了摇头。

欢迎来到地狱。
我们有两个墓地,没有医院。
请小心驾驶。

The Road through Hell

By David Cairns

"Slow down!"

"Why?" said Pete, easing his foot off the accelerator slightly. "It's three o'clock in the bloody morning. The coppers are asleep. Gimme that bottle!"

"It's dangerous," replied his long suffering girlfriend, Kelly, before reluctantly handing him the bottle. She was used to his penchant for speeding and criminal disregard for safety. An urgent reminder in the form of loud verbal abuse was usually all it took to bring him back into line, even if it never lasted very long.

"It's so dark," she said.

"It's night time, stupid!" They always travelled at night. In fact they did everything at night. She didn't really know why, it was just the way they were. Living a life of occasional highs under a smothering blanket of darkness. A sign appeared on the left of the narrow highway, shining briefly in the unearthly glare of the headlights. Kelly read it out loud in a tone of forced interest, as she often did, mocking Debra Winger's senile father in *Forget Paris*.

> *Welcome to Hell.*
> *A New South Wales tidy town.*
> *pop. 653*

"Wanna spend a night in Hell honey?" "Why don't you drive right on through to Heaven instead?" said Kelly, trying to sound flippant. She had never felt more afraid and it wasn't just the name of the town. A shadow moved on to the road ahead, and stayed out in front of them for a few seconds. Then it disappeared. Did she imagine it? It returned, quickly growing as though inflated by an invisible compressor, and began to form into a ragged sphere. What was it? Could Pete see it?

She pointed but Pete was already looking, straining for a better view. "What the hell was that?" He flicked the high beams off, then on again to see if it was a trick of light. No trick. The shape grew larger still and was soon joined by another, then another. Pete gripped the wheel in panic, his blood starved hands shared a ghostly luminescence which shone on his face but he did not slow down. "Is it an animal? I can't see. I can't tell!"

Kelly was frozen, suffocating behind a mask of awful terror as she watched a third shape ooze up from underneath the road. The three things maintained their speed and kept themselves just in front of the car before suddenly merging into one. The new shapeless entity was bigger than the car.

As they stared in dumb horror, a huge misshapen head extended from the centre of the black formless mass, followed quickly by two arms, then two long and powerful legs. It was running! Kelly screamed as it turned to look over its shoulder at them. Accompanied by a wide toothless smile, two bloodshot eyeballs floated in a sea of torn flesh, gawking mischievously.

Madness gripped Pete, insane fear drove him to press harder on the accelerator as the monstrous apparition turned its whole hulking frame to face them. Still running, backwards now, it laughed at them. "I'll kill you, get off the road, I'll kill you!" roared Pete. "I'll kill you, get off the road, I'll kill you!" mimicked the beast, its disturbingly deep and raspy voice amplified inside the car.

In the same instant that the running creature put up his open palmed hands and stopped dead in the middle of the road, the car crashed into a tree and split in two. Flung like worthless trash, the twisted halves of metal and plastic sped through the cold night air in opposite directions, carrying human debris with them. The crumpled bodies of the young couple were discovered the next morning, on either side of a sign post which stood like a sentinel in a grassy field. The doctor rose from his knees and nodded to the police sergeant who pulled a blanket over the face of the woman. He looked at the sign and sadly shook his head.

Welcome to Hell.

We have two graveyards and no hospitals.

Please drive carefully.

哈里欧姆老年中心

[印度]里纳·沙阿

宝宝说这里更好些。陪伴多，关照多，擦洗、喂饭和翻身也多一些。一键按下去，床既可以下降也可以上升，还能够更换浸透尿渍的床单。

我说没关系，你走吧。去参加派对，做做瑜伽，好好工作。可穿短裙的话只会给你惹麻烦。

多数时候，我醒来就能闻见茜拉那双大凉鞋的味道，而她还在我旁边的床上打着震天响的呼噜。我屏息静气以提防被熏死。真倒霉啊！

周二是河神的祭日。她们会把我们推到公共休息室，盯着简易的庙宇看。毗湿奴那么小，就像是希夫的替身舞者。我面对着所谓的花园，实际上就是个停车场。有人给了我几个手指铙钹，这样我就可以为跑调的祈祷歌添加些配乐。

为了占据最佳视野，护士们排列成马吉块状站在前面。我确信在我大声嚷嚷之前她们会转过身来的。轻轻的一声"汪汪"。曼塔抬起下巴又垂了下去。乔蒂开始打钹。

我又大声嚷嚷了一下。这次声音大了一点，给护士们带来了小小的干扰。双臂多毛的盖亚那抬头看了看，盯着餐厅。曼塔依旧弓着腰。

乔蒂像个蹒跚学步的小孩似的拍着铙钹。

当护士们再次不注意时,我又咆哮了一声。盖亚那露出不悦的神色,双手放在宽大的臀部上。这一次眼睛落在我身上。我拿起铙钹,加入到音乐当中去。

周二也是耆那教午餐日。禁食洋葱,禁食大蒜,禁食姜,也禁了好胃口。凯坦娶了他称之为"亲爱的荷娜"的耆那教女子。三十年来,我一直暗暗地恨着她。

餐盘端上来的时候我看都没看,因为周二也是宝宝从曼哈顿来看我的日子。她做了场大秀,给盖亚那送礼物,用新盒子装着旧服装首饰,然后把我推到假花园里。"妈咪!看看你多么闪耀啊!"说得好像太阳不是天天升起来似的。

宝宝认为我是个圣人,她的妈咪总是很平和,因为这一辈子我都是笑对人生,说着没问题。为了去美国而典当首饰?没问题。为爱结婚?没问题。用发臭的橄榄油代替优质酥油来做吃的?没问题。

我听见她有时和那个夜夜酗酒的婆罗门丈夫打电话,翻来覆去就是聊黑牌威士忌。她说希望能再有间卧室。我希望我能更多地记住他们的谈话。可至少我还有那个盖亚那,能让我坐在犹太区的电视房里,胳膊举起、放下的动作像是愚蠢的猴子。

宝宝觉得我总是微笑,但其实是因为我的假牙太大了,根本闭不上嘴。

今天宝宝给我带了我最爱的吃的——牛油果吐司,上面撒上美沙拉。我袖手旁观,等着宝宝不耐烦地开始祈求我,一直到牛油果变成不能吃的棕色的烂泥。

但她根本没注意到。"阿米,你都不知道运气有多差。"她说道,告诉我凯坦要离婚了。再也没有耆那教的媳妇了?我的心脏轻轻跳了一

愿你历尽沧桑　内心安然无恙

跳，嘴角抽搐着，几乎要笑了。但宝宝满怀希望地看着我。可谁在意凯坦和那个大嗓门、在家庭聚会时还坐在他腿上的女人离婚呢？我像个聋哑人似的盯着吐司，宝宝都快哭了。

宝宝一走，我就赶在盖亚那把我推走前火速吃掉吐司。

回到屋里，茜拉正在修指甲。像是个大电影明星。像她跟我不一样，没穿戴尿不湿内裤似的，我拖着这双废腿戴尿不湿已有八年了。她画着口红，好像她的脸和我们的不一样，不会吓着小孩似的。她像大袋装粮食似的，只能整天待在屋里。

晚上她总紧握着钻石吊坠。谁也不知道她为什么不把这些钻石给她的女儿们。难不成是戴给我看？婊子。我从来不骂人，可现在我骂了她。我看着杂志上真实的、和茜拉一样的女人们，就是我不让宝宝在高中时看这些杂志。她们挤压着又小又硬的乳头。

睡前我会给茜拉讲故事。护士们为了让食物更美味，在鸡汤里添加佐料。要是医疗补助没及时到账的话，她们会把你丢到人行道上的。

茜拉的眼睛越来越圆，像是无知的婴儿。

明天，我就不这么做了。不嘲笑茜拉，不吃宝宝带来的吃的。总罢工又复工了。

可今晚，我会像在路边生孩子一样大声嚷嚷。像我和凯坦、宝宝这样自大的人都会死。她将我撕裂，而我依旧抱着她。

盖亚那冲了进来。我低头假装睡觉，所以她朝着茜拉叫喊。"你是怎么回事？为什么这么吵？你会吵醒那些困倦的女士的。"我听到茜拉的呜咽声，心中感到小小的快乐。

起初我在做梦，感觉我的胳膊和双腿被手拽着离开了床，我像是拉尼维多利亚。我好像又是少女了。响起的钟声像是孟买微风中的庙铃。就像苏西瓦拉在呼唤我的名字，跟我说他卖的秋葵和西红柿是最好的。他触摸我的手时是怎样的感觉啊!铃声叮当,响在我心房啊!

可我其实当时坐在轮椅上,双脚晃荡着,因为不知是谁忘了放搁脚板了。大半夜的我被推到了停车场,那里的天空是夜空蓝。

我看到了曼塔,我看到了拉西米和乔蒂,却没见盖亚那。就只有几个夜班护士像小鸟一样跑来跑去的。

公共休息室里满是烟雾。在不好的祭神河仪式上着了火。

我抓着扶手往后看。

茜拉呢?

消防车在哪儿?为什么没人泼水呢?咦,茜拉和那些燃烧着的塑料神还在里面呢。尽管我不在乎,可我胸口还是一阵疼痛。茜拉一个人还在那傻傻地睡着呢。因为查帕克喜欢河流,我们给宝宝取名瑞亚。在我们像雨水一样来了又去的婴儿夭折以后,瑞亚出生了。我张开嘴,仰起脸来对着月亮大声嚷嚷,仿佛它能听见一般。我看见了她,那个我亲手造的小鬼。

Hari Om Senior Center

By Reena Shah

Baby says here is better. More company. More care. More wipe and feed and roll to one side. Button to push for fall. Button to push for sit up in bed. For change sheets that stink of own urine.

I say no matter. You go. Be at party. Do hot yoga. Go to work. Wear short dress that only causes trouble.

Most days I wake up to smell of Sheela's big sandals while Sheela herself still snoring soundly in neighboring bed. I hold breath in case death needs help. No luck.

Tuesday is Aarti day. They wheel us out to common room to stare at cheap temple. Vishnu so tiny like back up dancer to Shiv. I face garden, which is really parking lot. Someone gives me finger cymbals so I can add noise to out-of-tune devotional singing.

Nurses line up lumpiest majis in front for best view. I make sure their backs are turned before I bark. Just tiny "woof". Mamta lifts chin from chest and drops it. Jyoti starts cymbaling.

I bark again. More howly this time. Cause small disturbance

at nurses' station. Guyanese with hairy arms looks up. Eyes dining room. Mamta still hunched. Jyoti clapping cymbals like toddler.

When nurses go back to paying no attention I growl. Guyanese puts hands on wide hips and scowls. This time, eyes settle on me. I pick up cymbals and join cling clang.

Tuesday is also Jain lunch day. No onion, no garlic, no ginger. No taste. Ketan married to Jain woman who he calls "Honey-Hona". Thirty years I hate her quietly.

When lunch tray comes I don't even look because Tuesday is also when Baby visits from Manhattan. She makes big show and gives gifts to Guyanese, old costume jewelry in new boxes, then rolls me out to fake garden. "Mommy! Look how sunny for you!" As if sun does not rise every day.

Baby thinks I am saint, that her mommy is all calm because whole life I smile and say no problem. Sell gold bangles to go to America? No problem. Want love marriage? No problem. Make food with stinking olive oil instead of wholesome ghee? No problem.

I hear her on phone sometimes with Brahmin husband who drinks every night. Black label-flack label. Says she wishes they had extra bedroom. Wishes I remembered more. How at least I have Guyanese who makes sure I sit in TV room in Jewish section and do arm up/arm down like stupid monkeys.

Baby thinks I'm always smiling but really fake teeth are just too big to properly close mouth.

Today Baby brings my favorite treat—avocado toast topped with methi masala. I fold my arms and wait for Baby to start fussing and begging until avocado turns to sad brown mush.

But she hardly takes notice. "Ammi, you won't believe our luck," she says and tells me Ketan is getting divorce. No more Jain daughter-in-law? My heart gives small jump. My mouth twitches. I almost smile, and Baby looks at me hopeful. But who cares if Ketan no longer married to woman who talks too loud and sits on his lap during family parties? I stare at toast like a deaf/dumb and Baby nearly cries.

Once Baby leaves, I rush to eat toast before Guyanese wheels me away.

Back in room, Sheela is filing her nails. Like she big film star. Like her panties are not same diaper I tugged up crippled legs for eight years. She wears lipstick as if her face does not scare small children like rest of ours. Allowed to stay in room all day because she is like many sacks of grain.

At night she clutches diamond pendant in fist. Who knows why she does not give away all diamonds to daughters. To wear here for me? Bitch. Whole life I not curse and now I say bitch. I look at real Sheelas in filmy magazines, same magazines I not let Baby read in high school. Push on their small, hard nipples.

Before sleep, I tell Sheela stories. Nurses cook relish in chicken broth to make tasty. If Medicaid misses payment they put you on footpath.

Sheela's eyes grow round. Like infant with no knowledge.

Tomorrow, I'll stop. Stop taunting Sheela, Stop eating Baby's treats. Bandh. Finished.

But tonight I make big fat howl like having babies in the street. Bigheaded ones like Ketan and Baby and I will die. How she tore me open and still I held her.

Guyanese rushes in. I drop chin and fake sleep so instead she yells at Sheela. "What is wrong with you? Why you making such a ruckus? You'll wake up all these tired ladies." I hear Sheela whimper and feel small pleasure.

At first I am dreaming. Feel hands on my arms and legs lifting me out of bed like I am Rani Victoria. Like I am a girl again. Bells ringing like temple bells in Mumbai breeze. Like Subziwallah calling my name, telling me he has best okra and tomato for sale. How he touches my hand. How it rings and rings inside me.

But then I am in chair with feet dangling because whoever it is forgot footrest. Wheels me out to car park where sky is night blue.

I see Mamta. I see Laxmi and Jyoti. No Guyanese. Just night nurses who rush around like birds.

Smoke fills common room. Fire from no good aarti.

I grip armrest to look behind me.

Sheela?

Where are fire trucks? Why is no one throwing water? Why, when Sheela is still inside with melting plastic gods? Though I care not, I feel pain in chest. Sheela alone and stupidly asleep. Baby who we named Rhea because Champak loved rivers. Rhea, who was born after dead baby came and went like rains. I open my mouth and raise my face to the moon, howl like it can hear me. I see her, little ghost I made myself.

夺命来电

电话铃响了，卡尔从酣睡中醒来，接起了电话。他得到消息并通知了家属，他会在一小时之内到达。作为葬礼主管，这是他最不喜欢的一件事，他讨厌那些深夜来电，讨厌在梦中被惊醒，这似乎都让他不快，让他生气。他穿上朴素的职业装前往殡仪馆。他前天晚上就准备好了所有的尸体回收设备。

卡尔把地址输入定位系统中，给车的挡风玻璃解冻，他只有确定一切就绪时才会上路。清醒之后，他就很享受那种只有在深夜或大清早才有的安宁的驾驶时刻。

他到了死者的住处，情况看起来都很正常。有几辆车停在那里。他以为会有个护士在现场，但是很奇怪，现场没有护士。卡尔走进屋里，跟这家的家属打了招呼，问了谁是负责人，他应该跟谁谈。一个女人说护士已经走了。他被引见给死者的妻子海伦。他向海伦表示了同情和哀悼，请求她带自己到死者身边。他核实了他要接的死者姓名：罗伯特·佩顿。"佩顿太太，您已经瞻仰过遗容了吗？"卡尔问。她点了点头，想和其他家庭成员商量一下，以确定已经做好罗伯特被殡仪馆主管带走的准备。

他没办法在晚上这个时候把其他人从床上弄出来，这是单独行动。谢天谢地，这没有楼梯，罗伯特也不是很重。事实上，他看起来很年轻、很健康。卡尔以前也遇到过这种情况，慢性疾病几乎对人的身体外形没有什么影响。他什么都没想，大脑里唯一的念头就是把这个人安全体面地运出家门。

　　家属也来帮忙把罗伯特抬上停尸床，卡尔把他盖起来，向搬运车走去。罗伯特上车后车门就关上了。卡尔回去问家属有关后事安排的事。一进门，家属就告诉他罗伯特要火葬，没有任何服务项目，什么也没有。"明白了，我们明天上午10点见面好吗？"他说。海伦同意了。"我需要统计一些重要信息，你很容易回答的，需要他的法定全名，你需要他的名字怎么出现在讣告中，还有他父母的名字和参军记录等。"

　　"这些我们都有，明天见面的时候我把这些都告诉你。"海伦说。"还有什么问题吗？没有我就走了。"卡尔说。"没有了，谢谢你做的一切。"海伦说。卡尔和大家一一握手，离开了这幢房子。他上了车，恭敬而得体地把车开走了。卡尔开始驾驶，慢慢放松，打开了音乐。他开始注意到晚上开车是多么宁静平和。回殡仪馆的路上，他安顿妥当，心情开始放松。卡尔听到停尸床"吱吱"作响，他什么都没想，在一辆移动的车里，这太司空见惯了。

　　卡尔感到有什么东西缠在他的手臂上。他回头看，是一只手。卡尔大吃一惊，跳了起来，结果用力过猛，安全带划破了他的身体，他的背部、颈部都感觉疼痛不堪，锁骨断裂。他惊慌失措，无法集中注意力开车，迎面撞上了一辆半挂车。车的前端撞上了半挂车，就像正面撞到了一面混凝土墙一样。车窗玻璃碎了，像剃刀一样飞过货车。这一撞导致他的器官破裂，脖子也折断了，几乎当场要了卡尔的命。罗伯特被甩到座位间的仪表盘上，头骨塌陷。两人双双丧命。

Death Calls

The phone rang. Kal woke from a deep sleep and answered it. He got the information and told the family he would be there within the hour. This was one thing Kal didn't like about being a funeral director. He hated the late night calls and being woke from a deep sleep. It seemed to jar him and make him ill. He put on his pristine professional attire headed to the funeral home. All the body retrieval equipment was in place from his preparation the night before.

Kal punched the address of the decedent into his GPS and started to defrost his windshield. Once he made sure he had everything, he was on his way. Once awake he enjoyed the peaceful drive that was only allowed by late nights or very early mornings.

He arrived at the residence and things looked very normal. There were several cars parked there. He assumed there was a nurse on the scene. Oddly there wasn't. Kal walked in the house and he greeted the family and asked who was in charge and who he needed to speak with. A woman said the nurse had already left. He was introduced to the wife of the deceased: Helen. He extended his sympathy to Helen and offered his condolences and asked to be taken to where the deceased was. He verified the name of the person he was to pick up: Robert Peyton. "Mrs. Peyton, have you taken all the time you need?" Kal said. She nodded her head and wanted to check with the other family members to make sure Robert was ready to be taken away by the funeral director.

He wasn't able to get anyone else out of bed at that hour of the night. This was a solo operation. Thankfully there wasn't any stairs and Robert wasn't heavy at all. In fact, he appeared to be very young and looked healthy. Kal had seen this sort of thing before in this business. Diseases and chronic conditions can do almost anything to human physiology. He thought nothing about it. The only thing on his mind was to get this person out of the house safety and respectfully.

Family members helped get Robert onto the cot and Kal covered him up and began to head out the door to the removal van. Once Robert was in the van and the door shut Kal went back in to ask the family about arrangements. Once inside the family told him Robert was to be cremated and there were to be no services at all; nothing. "Understood, can we meet tomorrow morning at 10?" he said. Helen agreed. "I'll need vital statistic information that you'll likely be able to answer easily. You' need to have his full legal name, how you want his name in the obituary, mother and father's name and any military records."

"We have all of that. I'll have all the information with me tomorrow when we meet tomorrow," said Helen. "I'm going to head out unless you have any more questions for me," said Kal. "Okay, thank you for everything." Helen said. Kal shook everyone's hand and left the house. He got into the van and pulled away gracefully and respectfully. Kal settled into driving, started to relax and turned on some music. He started to notice how quiet and peaceful driving at night is. He settled in and began to relax while heading back to the funeral home. Kal heard the cot squeaking. He didn't think anything about it. It was a frequent thing when in a moving car.

Kal felt something wrap around his arm. He looked back. It was a hand. Kal was very startled and jumped with such force the seatbelt cut into his body. He felt pain in his back, neck and felt his collarbone snap. While in a sheer panic unable to focus on his driving he ran headlong into a semi. The front end of the van hit the semi as it would have hit a concrete wall head on. Glass shattered and flew through the van like flying razors. The impact ruptured organs and snapped his neck killing Kal almost instantly. Robert was flung over the console between the seats and his head hit the dash and caved in his skull. Both men were killed.

失落的记忆

[美国]托马斯·施密特

警探格雷格·华伦站在不再僵直的尸体旁边，尸体就在麦格雷格酒吧和烧烤餐厅的后门入口，非常血腥，很难辨认出是一个男人。他在尸体旁弯下腰，用手电照着尸体，想看得更清楚些。死者的胡须遮盖了过早长皱纹的脸，可以看出他生活艰难。华伦努力地想认出这个人，但巷子里灯光昏暗，很难辨认出更多的特征。

"我们最好把他送到停尸房，这样法医才可以验尸。"他对身后的警员说道。"看得出来他曾经被人狠狠地揍过。"

华伦闪到一边，救护车停了下来，急救医生拉出轮床。这些专业人员小心翼翼地把尸体放到轮床上，抬到了车里。车里的灯照亮了死者的脸，能看出他实际上是一个30岁出头的人。当华伦最后看清受害者的时候，他惊呆了。

"停！等一分钟。"华伦拉开救护车的后门走进去。不可能。真的不可能。

但是，事实确实如此。躺在轮床上的那具尸体是卢克·约瑟夫，华伦谢尔比维尔高中的同学。从高中毕业以后，华伦就再也没见过他。在毕业典礼上，卢克·约瑟夫因为各种行为问题被开除。他一直是高中恶霸，他的所作所为在那天终于得到了惩罚。

约瑟夫的生活怎么变成了这个样子？肯塔基州谢尔比维尔市的某个人出了什么问题吗？杀人只是其中的一部分？要么这是约瑟夫与路易斯维尔或者圣路易斯暴徒勾结的结果？华伦心中疑窦丛生，却找不出答案。

"我跟你们一块儿去郡停尸房。"他对急救医务人员说。医务人员点了点头，关上了救护车后门。格雷格·华伦是个出了名的爱冲动、感情用事的人，所以往往很容易卷入他的案子。尽管这些急救医生不知道这个，但是对他来说这个特别的案子是有个人性质的。

救护车驶向郡停尸房的途中，华伦拿手电继续观察约瑟夫的尸体。他想想起这个人，但很难记起有关约瑟夫的具体细节。高中期间，约瑟夫有自己的小团队，多数时候都是冷漠的。他做了什么被开除的？华伦想不起来了。

救护车开进谢尔比维尔停尸房，停在了后坡上。医务人员搬下轮床，把尸体推到停尸房安置区。填完必要的与尸体有关的文件后，医务人员把轮床推回1号尸检室，留下华伦跟死者卢克·约瑟夫。华伦还在盯着约瑟夫的脸，一直在想从高中以后这个人过的是什么样的生活。

几分钟后，有人推开了尸检室的门，华伦还在沉思。法医罗伯特·普雷斯科特走了进来，穿着手术服准备解剖尸体。离房间不远时他停住了，周四晚上10点看见华伦在这儿让他觉得很惊讶。

"没在家看电视吗，华伦？"法医边往华伦警探那边走边问。"想不出为什么工作日的晚上你会待在这儿而不在家里。"

"打扰了，罗伯特，"警探回答道，"但是这个人我认识。我高中同学。"

"推测出发生了什么吗？"法医开始检查尸检台上尸体的时候问

道。他脱掉死者的衬衫和裤子,方便用眼睛给尸体做一个由面部到全身的检查。

"不太清楚。只是看起来他遭到了毒打。"

"确实是这样。"普雷斯科特检查着尸体,同时记录着他最初的肉眼尸检发现。"听着,格雷格。你为什么不今晚先回家,明天上午10点左右再来呢?我做尸检和毒理检测是需要时间的。明天早上我才能告诉你更多信息。"

"好的,罗伯特。我知道你做这些需要时间。"

华伦在第二天早上10点来到停尸房,急切地想听听罗伯特·普雷斯科特对卢克·约瑟夫的发现。他在接待区看见了打着哈欠煮咖啡的法医。

"昨晚有新发现吗?"

"实际上,我发现了很多。接杯咖啡,让我们谈一谈死者约瑟夫先生吧。"

普雷斯科特医生开始概述尸检中的发现。卢克·约瑟夫头部、胸部和背部有创伤。面部和上胸部有严重淤青,还伴有开放性伤口。此外,毒理检测发现约瑟夫血液中含有可卡因,酒精检测为0.22%,远远高于醉酒标准。

"约瑟夫头天晚上离开酒吧的时候喝得酩酊大醉,所以可能很难看清袭击者们,更不要说保护自己了。"

"罗伯特,你用了'袭击者们'这个词。你的意思是袭击卢克·约瑟夫的不止一人?"

"是这样,没错。约瑟夫尸体上的淤青有手指印,说明有人用手抓着他。淤青上有两套不同的指纹。一个手大一点,另一个相对较小。"

"哇,你这条信息让我大吃一惊。"

普雷斯科特喝了一小口咖啡说道:"你知道吗,这起谋杀案跟我们上周接到的谢尔比维尔北部的一起案子有很多相似点。"

华伦不再记笔记,顿住抬头看着罗伯特·普雷斯科特:"哪起谋杀案?"

普雷斯科特用手摸着下巴,然后说道:"13号的时候我们接收过谢尔比维尔北部送来的一具尸体。尸体的脸部、胸部和背部都有淤青,就跟这具尸体一样。但更重要的是,那具尸体的淤青上的指纹也跟这具尸体的一样。一些是大手的,一些是小手的。"

华伦想了一下这个信息,然后问下一个问题:"知道谢尔比维尔北部受害者的身份了吗?"

普雷斯科特又喝了一口咖啡,然后说道:"知道,那个人来自兰开斯特,名叫哈罗德·埃利奥特,32岁。"

华伦坐在那,脸色变得苍白,他感到难以置信。那个人可能是谢尔比维尔高中的"比弗·埃利奥特"吗??又一个同学?如果是这样的话,这一切就都不是巧合了。

华伦上学的时候,哈罗德"比弗"埃利奥特是谢尔比维尔高中足球队的队长。他是那个高中受欢迎人群中的一个,自负又傲慢,本身有点横行霸道。也许这就是他跟卢克·约瑟夫玩得好的原因吧。他们在同一个圈子里一起旅行。他们是"朋友",甚至直呼彼此的大名。华伦终于记起了有关这两个人的一些细节。

华伦的大脑一边思考,一边转身问了罗伯特·普雷斯科特最后一个问题:"尸检中你对卢克·约瑟夫和哈罗德·埃利奥特还有其他发现吗?"

普雷斯科特点了点头,放下咖啡杯,说:"有。两具尸体都有另外一个非同寻常的状况。两人头部的右侧头发都被剪了,头皮有伤口和出血。两具尸体的伤痕非常相似。"

华伦闭上眼睛，左手撑住了耷拉下来的头。噢，我的天哪！他脑海中闪过的想法让他头晕目眩，脊背发凉。

"你还好吗？格雷格？"普雷斯科特从椅子上起身向华伦走去，嘴里问道。这个警探看起来像是生病了。

"我觉得我大概知道谋杀者是些什么人了。他们的杀人行动还没有结束，他们的杀人名单上应该还有另一个人。"

罗伯特·普雷斯科特一脸狐疑地看着格雷格·华伦给谢尔比维尔警局打电话。他没法听清说的大部分是什么，但是听见华伦说"就这么做"和"在这个案子上相信我"。打完电话后，华伦感谢普雷斯科特给的尸检报告，开车走了。

开车到镇外的布福德农场只花了20多分钟。这个老旧的农场一片漆黑，但是华伦还是走了过去。拔出枪，格雷格·华伦走进正屋，门没关着，他蹑手蹑脚地上了楼梯。

角落里的卧室亮着一盏昏暗的灯，门微微欠了个缝。华伦环顾四周，慢慢地推开门。屋里传来一个声音，轻轻地对他喊道："进来吧，警探，我一直在等你。"

华伦打开顶灯，走进房间。一个小个子男人坐在摇椅上，面朝屋子的前窗。旁边的床上躺着一个高个子男人，衣服被血染红。华伦很快认出那是约翰·布福德，他家里人管他叫"小约翰"，他已经死了。他的哥哥山姆还在他旁边的摇椅上摇着。

"你为什么要这么做，山姆？"虽然已经知道答案了，华伦还是明知故问。"你为什么要杀了卢克·约瑟夫和哈罗德·埃利奥特？"

华伦在等待答案，而山姆·布福德还在摇。"你知道答案的，格雷格。你应该清楚。整个高中，约瑟夫和埃利奥特都在折磨我和约翰。他们以打我们为乐,取笑约翰的学习障碍。他们甚至剪掉了我们的一部分头发,管头发叫'战利品',来取笑我们的印第安人血统。你们其余的人都只是围观,什么都不做。"

华伦羞愧地低下头,这些话让他心烦意乱。布福德声称他对当年霸凌行为持消极态度,他无法否认,难辞其咎。

"山姆,我可以理解你对我们的愤怒,但是为什么要杀了约翰?"

布福德耸了耸肩,继续摇着摇椅,说:"我不得不这样做。约翰会被折磨,甚至很有可能在我们审判后,在监狱里被强奸。其他的囚犯会叫他智障,虐待他。我不得不保护他,让他免受这些罪。"

华伦带着遗憾和疑虑的复杂心情看着山姆,说:"一切都结束了,山姆。我已经派人去了 JT 劳伦斯的家。你没法靠近他了。"

JT 劳伦斯,是"三兄弟"中的最后一位,也是高中这个三人帮的头儿。人长得帅,受人欢迎,会对大人花言巧语,他现在是谢尔比维尔县政府的议员。华伦确定他是布福德的最后一个目标。

"太晚了,格雷格,劳伦斯今天早上就已经死了。我和约翰为了结束这一切已经把他杀了。"

华伦沮丧地垂下头,看着布福德继续摇晃着椅子。他能做些什么来阻止这一切的发生呢?他应该做些什么呢?他知道这些问题的答案都要追溯到过去,16 年前。

布福德不再摇椅子了,他转过身,面对华伦道:"带走我吧,格雷格,你还要尽你对国家的职责。"说着这些,他走向华伦,伸出双臂,做好了戴手铐的准备。

Forgotten Memories

By Thomas Schmidt

Detective Greg Warren stood over the limp body laying beside the back entrance to McGregor's Bar and Grill. Dirty and bloody, it was hard to believe that this was once a man. He stooped down beside the body so that he could shine his light on the man to get a better view. The beard on the man covered the premature wrinkling of a face that had seen a hard life. Warren tried hard to recognize the man but the dim lighting in the alley made it difficult to make out many features.

"We'd better get him to the morgue so that the ME can examine the body," he said to the uniformed officers standing behind him. "It looks like he was beat to a pulp by someone."

As Warren moved aside, the ambulance pulled up and the EMTs brought out a gurney. The techs carefully placed the body on the gurney and lifted it into the open van. The interior lighting illuminated the man and showed him to actually be someone who was probably in his early 30's. Warren froze as he finally got a closer look at the victim.

"Stop! Hold up for a minute." Warren pulled open the back door of the ambulance and got right in. It couldn't be. It just couldn't be.

But it was. Lying on the gurney was the body of Luke Joseph, a classmate of Warren's from Shelbyville High. Warren hadn't seen the man since high school graduation, a graduation that Luke Joseph had been tossed out of due to various behavioral issues at that event. Luke Joseph had been the high school bully and his actions finally caught up with him on that day.

How had Joseph's life come to this? Was the killing part of something that had gone wrong with someone from the small town of Shelbyville, Kentucky? Or was this possibly the result of Joseph's involvement with thugs from Louisville or perhaps St. Louis? Warren had a lot of questions and no answers.

"I'm riding with the body to the county morgue," he said to the emergency medical technicians. The men nodded and simply closed the van's door. Greg Warren was known to be a driven, impulsive man so it was not unusual for him to get heavily involved in some of his cases. And although the med techs didn't know it, this particular case was personal to him.

Warren once again illuminated Joseph's body as the ambulance made its way to the county morgue. He tried to remember the man but had trouble bringing back any specific memories about Joseph.

While in high school, Joseph had kept to a small group of friends and was aloof in many ways. What had he done to get toss from his graduation? Warren couldn't remember.

The ambulance entered the Shelbyville County morgue and parked at the back ramp. The techs removed the gurney and wheeled the body into the morgue receiving area. After filling out the necessary paperwork for the body, the EMTs pushed the gurney back to Examining Room 1 where they left Warren and the deceased Luke Joseph. Warren continued to look at Luke Joseph's face, all the time wondering what kind of life this man had had since high school.

Warren was still deep in thought when the examining room door opened a few minutes later. Medical Examiner Robert Prescott came in, fully gowned and ready to work on the body. He stopped a short distance into the room, surprised to see Greg Warren in the room at 10 PM on a Thursday night.

"Don't have cable Warren?" the cocky ME asked as he walked up to the detective. "Can't think of any other reason why you would be here instead of at home on a weeknight."

"Sorry to impose Rob," the detective replied. "But this one is personal. Went to high school with the man."

"Any idea what happen?" the ME asked as he started to look at the body on the examination table. He pulled off the dead man's shirt and pants while extending his visual examination from the face to the man's full body.

"Not really. Just looks like he was beaten severely."

"That he was." Prescott continued to examine the body while taking notes on his initial visual impressions of the corpse. "Look, Greg. Why don't you go home for the evening and come back mid-morning tomorrow. It will take me a while to do an autopsy and tox screen. I'll be able to tell you more in the morning."

"OK Rob. I know you need some time to do your work."

Warren was back in the morgue at 10 AM the next morning, anxious to hear what Rob Prescott had found out about Luke Joseph. He caught the ME yawning in the reception area while making coffee.

"Learn anything more overnight?"

"Actually, I learned a lot. Grab yourself some coffee and let's have a talk about the departed Mr. Joseph."

Prescott proceeded to outline what he had found in his examination. Luke Joseph had suffered trauma to his head, chest, and back. The bruising was severe with some open wounds being present particular in the face and upper chest. In addition, Prescott's tox screen found cocaine in Joseph's blood and an alcohol level of 0.22%, well above the intoxication level.

"Joseph was so drunk when he left the bar last night that he probably had trouble seeing his attackers much less defending himself."

"Rob, you used the term 'attackers'. Do you believe Luke Joseph was attacked by more than one man?"

"Yes, definitely. Joseph's body has bruising patterns on it that show finger marks from the hands holding him. Two different sets of finger patterns are in the bruising. One is from large hands and the other from much smaller hands."

"Wow. You surprised me with that information."

Prescott took a small sip from his coffee and then continued. "You know, this murder has some similarities to the one we had in North Shelbyville last week."

Warren stopped writing notes and looked up at Rob Prescott. "What murder?"

Prescott stroked his chin before responding. "We had a body come in from North Shelbyville on the 13th. The corpse had bruising in the face, chest and back just like this one. But more importantly, the bruising also showed some of the same type of finger patterns on the body. Some from large hands, others from smaller ones."

Warren gave the information some thought before asking his next question. "Any ID on the North Shelbyville victim?"

Prescott took another sip of coffee and then replied. "Yes, the man was Harold Elliott from Lancaster. 32 years old."

Warren's face turned white as he sat in disbelief. Could the man be "Biff Elliott" from Shelbyville High?? Another classmate? If so, then all of this just could not be a coincidence.

Harold "Biff" Elliott had been the Shelbyville High football team captain while Warren attended the school. He was part of the popular crowd at Shelbyville High. Conceded and arrogant, Biff was a bit of the bully himself. Perhaps that is why he got along so well with Luke Joseph. They travelled together in the same circle. They were "amigos" and even called each other by the name. Warren finally was remembering some details about the two men.

Warren's mind was racing as he turned back to Rob Prescott to ask one final question. "Did you find anything else in your examination of Luke Joseph and Harold Elliott?"

Prescott nodded and put down his coffee cup. "Yes. Both corpses had one other unusual condition. Both men had hair removal on the right side of their heads, with cuts and bleeding on the scalp. The appearance on both bodies was very similar."

Warren dropped his head into his left hand as he closed his eyes. Oh my god. Chills went up his spine as he got faint from the thoughts going through his mind.

"You OK Greg?" Prescott got up from his chair and walked over to Warren. The police detective looked ill.

"I think I may know who did these murders. And they may have one more person on their list to kill before they're through."

Rob Prescott watched inquisitively as Greg Warren talked on his cell phone to the Shelbyville County Police. He couldn't make out much of the conversation but he did hear Warren say "just do it" and "trust me on this". When the call was done, Warren thanked Prescott for his examination work and took off toward his car.

The drive to the Bufford farm just outside of town only took slightly more than 20 minutes. The old farm was dark but Warren approached it nonetheless. With his gun drawn, Greg Warren entered the unlocked door of the main house and tiptoed up the stairs.

A dim light was on in the corner of bedroom and the door was slightly ajar. Warren opened it slowly as he looked around. A voice from inside the room softly called out to him. "Come in detective, I have been expecting you."

Warren turned on an overhead light and entered the room. A small man was sitting in a rocking chair and facing the front window of the room. On the bed beside him was a large man with blood stained clothes. Warren quickly realized that John Bufford, "Little John" as he was called by his family, was dead. His brother Sam continued to rock on the chair beside him.

"Why did you do it Sam?" Warren asked even though he already knew the answer. "Why did you kill Luke Joseph and Biff Elliott?"

Sam Bufford continued to rock as Warren waited for a reply. "You know the answer Greg. It should be clear to you. Joseph and Elliott tormented John and me all through high school. They got their kicks out of punching us, making fun of John's learning disabilities. They even cut off parts of our hair, calling it 'scalping' to make fun of our Native American heritage. And all the rest of you just stood around and did nothing about it."

Warren looked down in shame as the words ate into him. He couldn't deny Bufford's claims about his passiveness to the bullying.

"Sam, I understand your anger toward us but why kill John?"

Bufford shrugged as he continued to rock in the chair. "Had to. John would have been tormented, possibly even raped in prison after our trial. The other inmates would have called him retarded and abused him. I had to protect him from all of that."

Warren looked at Sam with a mixture of pity and disbelief. "It's over Sam. I have people at JT Lawrence's house. You won't get to him."

JT Lawrence, the last of the "Three Amigos", was the leader of the three man gang in high school. Good looking, popular, and a con-artist with adults, JT was now a councilman in the Shelbyville County government. Warren was sure that he was the last of Bufford's targets.

"Too late Greg. Lawrence has been dead since this morning. John and I killed him to finish this work."

Warren dropped his head in frustration as he watched Bufford continue to rock. What could he have done to prevent all of this from occurring? What should he have done? He knew that the answer to those questions were back in the past.16 years in the past.

Bufford stopped rocking, turned around and faced Warren. "Take me in Greg. You still have your duty to the county to perform. " With that, the man approached Warren, his arms extended and ready to be cuffed.

脑洞大开的实验

[美国] 麦克·克拉斯

罗伯特告诉妻子:"现在,我要出趟远门了。你会几年都看不到我,可我最终会回来看你。"

"你要去哪里?"

"我要进入未来。当你再看到我的时候,我肯定你会生气,可不会太久,因为我一旦看到你,我那时会再次消失。从现在开始,你只能看到我在这里站立五分钟了。"

罗伯特的妻子大惑不解。

他说:"我很好奇,如果我选择某种投资后置之不理,咱们的退休账户会是怎样的?我已经决定进入未来,离开二十年,看看结果。"

"你要是回不来可怎么办?"

他稍微顿了顿……接着说:"我希望,我做出的是正确的选择。"

"晚饭你想吃什么?"

"我现在不想给自己做任何安排,可是,五分钟后,我会告诉你我想要什么。"

罗伯特转身奔地下室而去。他的妻子还是一脸蒙,不过她知道罗伯特是个让人费解的人,便不管丈夫要不要,都去厨房做晚餐。她不太明白这都是什么意思。而五分钟以后,她很快就忘记了这次谈话的内容。

那天下午晚些时候,罗伯特的妻子走到地下室门口,敲了敲。她等着。她又敲了敲,没有回应。最后,她打开门,走进实验室。哪里都没有罗伯特的踪影。她没有听到他上去的声音。那他到哪里去了呢?

晚饭做好了,天光渐渐暗淡下来,罗伯特的妻子喊着他的名字,可是没人回答。屋子里十分安静。

"我不喜欢这样。"她心想,"他以前吃饭可从来没晚过。"

罗伯特的晚餐变凉了,他妻子把饭放进烤箱来保温,希望他回来的时候会注意到。第二天早晨,烤箱里罗伯特的盘子还是温的。他动也没动过。他妻子第二次寻找他,喊着他的名字,可是白费力气了——他不在家里。

几天后,罗伯特的妻子与官方联系,讲述了所发生的事情。他们在家里寻找线索,可是他们只在地下室的地板上发现了少量变色的斑点。

"他在离开前说过什么吗?"他们问。

"我在五分钟后回来。"她说。

官方离开了。又过了几天、几个星期、几个月后,这个案子就正式了结了。罗伯特失踪了,可是不能断定谋杀罪行,只能确认他只是抛弃了自己的妻子。罗伯特的妻子很不高兴。

几年过去了,罗伯特的妻子找到了一份工作,使她的生活保持在略微高于贫困线的水平。日复一日,她边干活,边诅咒丈夫离开了自己。她绝对不能原谅他。绝对不能!她的脸上的皱纹越来越多,曾经有过的明媚的笑颜已化作挥之不去的愁容。

终于,到了她丈夫离开正好二十年的那天。罗伯特的妻子坐在厨房的餐桌旁,这时听到了地下室传来声音。她立刻惊恐地站了起来。谁在下面?她听到有脚步声缓缓地走上台阶,最后,门打开了,出现在她的眼前的,不是别人,正是罗伯特。他看上去与离开的时候没什么两样。

"你!"她好不容易说出一句话来。

"好了,我们的退休账户值多少钱了?"罗伯特问。

"你到哪里去了?"

"这无关紧要。问题是退休账户的价值。我需要知道我的投资是否明智……"

"你二十年前离开我,没有留下一分钱过日子,现在还妄想退休账户有余额?"

"你全都花光了?"罗伯特问。"哦,了不起,真是了不起。我马上就要回去了。"

罗伯特转过身,走入地下室。

"罗伯特?罗伯特,你去哪里?"罗伯特的妻子说着,却突然看到一道耀眼的蓝色闪光,随后就什么都没有了。罗伯特又一次消失了。

罗伯特的妻子回到餐桌旁。她坐下来,努力回想所发生的一切。她心乱如麻,无法思考。退休账户已经——已经——她想起来了,从罗伯特离开后一直没有动,可是现在——她开始想起了其他问题。退休账户一直处于信托状态。根据信托条例,她二十年不能动这笔钱。随后,她想起当局曾经通知她,罗伯特已经抛弃了她,不知道他在哪里了。所以,只要她合法地宣布他已经死亡,从法律上讲信托资产是她的,不必等二十年了。

地下室又闪过一道亮光,脚步声传来,罗伯特走进厨房。

"值多少?"

"我已经告诉你了,我都花了。"

"我放入信托基金了。"

"我宣布你在法律上死亡了。"罗伯特的妻子说。

"哦,麻烦了。"罗伯特说。"我还得回去。"

一道亮光之后,罗伯特的妻子又一次蒙了。

"我说了我都花了吗?花什么了?"她想。罗伯特离开她后,她一直试图得到一些钱。她去查询退休账户剩下多少钱时,发现罗伯特把钱都取出来了,藏在什么地方——可是藏在哪里了呢?

又出现了一道光,罗伯特又到了厨房。

"你知道你让我遭了多少罪吗?你没有给我留下一分钱过日子。"

"这将全都是一个噩梦。"罗伯特说。

"如果不是我发现了后院埋藏的一些金币,我早就饿死了。"

"你发现了金币?"

"这么说,那里是你藏钱的地方!"罗伯特的妻子说。"好哇。我真高兴我发现了钱,还都花啦!"

罗伯特回到地下室,消失了。他的妻子静静地坐了一会儿,等着他出现,可他再没有回来。她站起身去做饭。她想到自己的丈夫,想保持对他的怨恨。她忽然想不出对他有什么可怨恨的。抛弃了她?可他从未抛弃过呀。她准是出现了幻想。她打开碗橱时,罗伯特走进了厨房。

"你决定晚饭吃什么了吗?"她问。"我还什么都没有做呢。"

"不用管我,我不饿。"罗伯特说着,坐在餐桌旁。

"怎么了?"

"这二十年,你那肮脏的双手不能不碰咱们的钱吗?"

"什么?"

"我才离开了不到二十年的时间,难道你就不能不把我们的钱都花了吗?"

"宝贝,你说什么呢?你离开只有五分钟啊,就有了让你困扰的事。"

罗伯特看着自己年轻时的妻子。

如果杀了她会怎样?他现在可以掐死她,进入未来,看退休账户会如何,在几分钟后回来,从此过上幸福生活。

"我能看一眼那条擦盘子的毛巾吗?"

罗伯特的妻子把擦盘子的毛巾递给他。使她绝望,让她大吃一惊的是,他用擦盘子的毛巾勒住她的脖子使她窒息,在这个过程中还一直告诉她:"别担心,这只是一个实验。"

罗伯特回到地下室,二十年后在一道闪光中再次出现了。

"谁在下面?"一个男人问着,走下地下室的台阶。

罗伯特没有想到这种情况。他想找地方躲藏,可是太晚了。房子的新主人有一支步枪。

"你祈祷吧。"

"等一等!我能解释清楚!"可是太晚了。罗伯特当时就被射中,向后倒下,彻底死亡——对于一个脑洞大开的实验来说,这是一个最凄惨的结局。

A Most Ambitious Experiment

By Mike Krath

"Now," Robert told his wife, "I am going on a long trip. You won't see me for years, but I will come back and see you."

"Where are you going?"

"I am going into the future. I am sure you will be angry when you see me, but it won't be for long, because once I have seen you, I will then vanish again and you will see me standing in this very spot exactly five minutes from now."

Robert's wife was puzzled.

"I am curious what our 401K will do if I invest in certain options and leave them," he said. "I've decided to go twenty years into the future and see the outcome."

"What if you can't come back?"

A slight pause-then, "I hope I made the right choice."

"What do you want for dinner?"

"I wouldn't make anything for me now, but, five minutes later, I will tell you what I want."

Robert left for the basement. His wife, still confused, but knowing that Robert was a puzzling man, went to the kitchen to make dinner, with or without her husband's request. She was quite unsure what to make of all of it, but, after a few minutes, she quickly forgot the conversation.

Later in the afternoon, Robert's wife walked over to the basement door and knocked. She waited. She knocked again, and, again, nothing. Finally, she opened the door and walked down to the laboratory. Robert was nowhere to be seen. She hadn't heard him come up. Where had he gone?

When supper was ready, and the light outside turned a dim color, Robert's wife called out his name, but no one answered. The house was quite still.

"I don't like this," she thought. "He's never been late for dinner before."

Robert's dinner grew cold, and his wife placed it in the oven to keep warm hoping he would notice it when he came back. In the morning, Robert's plate was still warm in the oven. He had never touched it. His wife looked for him once again and called out his name, but it was to no avail-he wasn't in the house.

After several days, Robert's wife contacted the authorities and told them what had happened. They searched the house for clues, but all they could find was a slightly discolored spot on the basement floor.

"Did he say anything before he left?" they asked.

"I'll be back in five minutes," she said.

After the authorities had left, and after several more days, weeks and months, the case was officially closed. Robert was missing, but since no foul play could be determined, it was decided that he had just deserted his wife. Robert's wife was not pleased.

Years passed, and Robert's wife was able to secure a job that kept her living slightly above poverty level. Day after day, while working, she cursed her husband for leaving her. She would never forgive him. Never! Her face became more wrinkled and the pretty smile she once wore turned into a permanent scowl.

Finally, twenty years to the day her husband had left, Robert's wife was sitting at the kitchen table when she heard a noise coming from the basement. She immediately got up in fright. Who was down there? She heard footsteps slowly walking up the stairs and finally the door flew open and there, before her eyes, was none other than Robert. He didn't look any different than when he had left.

"You!" she managed to say.

"Okay, what's the value of our 401K?" Robert asked.

"Where have you been?"

"That doesn't matter. What matters is the value of our 401K. I need to know if I invested wisely or not."

"You left me twenty years ago with nothing to live in and

expect to find anything left of the 401K?"

"You spent it all?" Robert asked. "Oh great, that's just great. I'll be right back."

Robert turned and went down into the basement.

"Robert? Robert, where are you?" Robert's wife said but suddenly saw a brilliant blue flash of light and then nothing. Robert had vanished once again.

Robert's wife went back to the dining table. She sat down and tried to think of what had happened. Her mind was muddled. She couldn't think. The 401K had been—had been—she thought—left untouched when Robert had first left, but now—she was beginning to remember different things. The 401K had been placed in a trust. A trust where she couldn't touch the money for twenty years. Then, she remembered that when the authorities had informed her that Robert had deserted her and was never located, that she had him declared legally dead so the trust would be legally hers without waiting for twenty years.

Another flash of light in the basement, more footsteps, and Robert walked into the kitchen.

"The value?"

"I told you I spent it."

"I put it in a trust."

"I had you declared legally dead." Robert's wife said.

"Oh bother," Robert said. "I'll be back again."

A flash of light and Robert's wife was again confused.

"Did I say spent it? Spent what?" she thought. She had tried to obtain some money after Robert had left her. When she had gone to inquire how much was in their 401K, she had found out that Robert had withdrawn the money and had hidden it somewhere-but where?

Another light and Robert was there in the kitchen again.

"Do you know how much you put me through? You left me nothing to live on."

"This will all be a bad dream," Robert said.

"If it wasn't for some gold coins that I found buried in the backyard, I would never have survived."

"You found the gold coins?"

"So that's where you hid the money!" Robert's wife said. "Good. I'm glad I found it and spent it all!"

Robert went back into the basement and disappeared. His wife sat still for a while expecting him to appear, but he never did. She got up and went to cook. She thought of her husband and tried to remain bitter against him. She suddenly couldn't think of what would make her bitter. Deserted her? He had never deserted. What an imagination she must have. As she opened a cupboard, Robert walked into the kitchen.

"Have you decided what you want for dinner?" she asked. "I haven't started making anything yet."

"Leave me alone, I'm not hungry," Robert said and sat down at the kitchen table.

"What's wrong?"

"Can't you keep your grubby hands off our money for twenty years?"

"What?"

"You can't let me leave you for a measly twenty years without spending everything we have, can you?"

"What are you talking about, honey? You haven't been gone for five minutes and already something is troubling you."

Robert looked at the wife of his youth.

What if he killed her? He could strangle her now, go into the future, see what the 401K did, come back a few minutes before, and live happily ever after.

"May I see that dish towel for a sec?"

Robert's wife handed it to him, and, much to her desperate surprise, he tied it around her neck and choked her, all the while telling her, "Don't worry, this is just an experiment."

Robert went back down into the basement, and twenty years later reappeared in a flash of light.

"Who's down there?" a man asked walking down the basement stairs.

Robert hadn't thought of this. He looked for somewhere to hide, but it was too late. The new owner of the house had a rifle.

"Say your prayers."

"Wait! I can explain!" But it was too late. Robert was immediately shot and fell backwards quite dead—a most miserable end to a most ambitious experiment.

密封的门

　　一定是他女儿干的。她想要她那份遗产,不然一个有钱人家的孩子为什么要杀人?然而,她的不在场证明是很确凿的。最重要的是,门是从里面锁上的,受害者的口袋里有钥匙。其中一幢维多利亚时代的老房子仍然用着原始的锁,需要钥匙才能进入每个房间。她说这是为了保持房子古老的魅力。我只觉得烦人,必须有一把钥匙才能进入每个房间,这太荒谬了。

　　这位父亲因脑部中弹死亡,这是自杀的经典选择,但特别奇怪的是,受害者的头部没有烧伤痕迹,这表明子弹发射时,枪不在他的头部附近。这告诉我,开枪打他的人与他之间有距离。但这仍然不能解释为什么门是从里面锁上的,以及钥匙为什么在受害人身上。据我所知,女儿没有备用钥匙,这座豪宅里也没有秘密通道。再说,枪是在受害人手里找到的,这也没什么用。

　　"如果你不需要我的话,"她说,"我现在可以离开吗?"该死。她还不能走。不能让她逃脱!等一下,我可能有主意了。我跑向尸体,看着在尸体上发现的钥匙。我仔细看了看,看到钥匙上有一条带子。我告诉其他警官搜查房子里所有的垃圾桶和废纸篓,然后他们带着我要找的东西回来了,还有一根长长的绳子。我走到他女儿跟前,邀请她到犯罪现场去。

"你想要一副手套吗?"我问。

"不。我讨厌戴手套。"

我笑了笑,然后走开了。

"伙计,你有没有听说过'密封门的把戏'?"

她直视着我的眼睛说:"没有。"

"让我来解释一下,"我说,"这是一个大多数人都已经淡忘了的把戏。因为现在大多数的门不需要钥匙就能锁上。若有一扇只能用钥匙从里面锁上的门,就很容易给人一种错觉,以为门是房间里的人锁上的。这只需要一根针、一根绳子和一些胶带就能做到。"

"怎么做呢?"她问。

"你先把绳子粘在钥匙上,然后你锁上门,把钥匙留在门上。然后你把绳子穿过门,将别人的口袋里的绳子系个圈,用针戳穿口袋,继续往前走,直到你再次走到门口为止。接下来,用从门下面伸出的绳子关上门。我们现在有一扇锁着的门,你是进不去的。然后你从门下面拉出绳子,让钥匙从锁里掉出来,把它串在房间的另一头,放进受害者的口袋里。然后你用力一拉,松开绳子,钥匙就留在了受害者的口袋里,给人一种钥匙自始至终都在受害者口袋里的错觉。"

她一脸茫然地看着我说:"天哪,那真是个把戏。"

"是的,鉴于这是你开枪打死你父亲后的所作所为。"

"探长,我没有杀我的父亲!"

"小姐,"我微笑着说,"带子上有你的指纹。"当我开始接近她时,她害怕地看着我。

"你讨厌戴手套这事真是太遗憾了。"

她继续盯着我,当我走到她面前时,她就像一只被车灯灯光罩住的鹿。

"我检查那卷带子时,尽管那只是其中一部分,我会在上面找到谁的指纹呢?"她羞愧地看着别处,双手举起来抱着胳膊。

"我能找到谁的指纹?"

"我的。"她最后说。

"谢谢你的诚实,"我抬头看着我的下属们说,"把她带走,告诉她她的权利。"

The Sealed Door

The daughter had to have done it. She wants her inheritance, why else would a rich kid commit murder? However, her alibi is solid and most importantly, the door was locked from the inside and the victim had the key in his pocket. One of those old Victorian homes that still has the original locks that require a key to get into each room. She says it was to keep the house's old charm, I just find it annoying. Having to have a key to get into each room is ridiculous.

The father died from a bullet to the brain, a classic choice for a suicide, but oddly enough, there are no burn marks on the victim's head, which states that the gun wasn't near his head when it went off. That tells me that whoever shot him was at a distance. But that still doesn't explain how the door was locked from the inside and the key on the victim's body. The daughter doesn't have a spare key and as far as I can tell, there are no secret passageways in this mansion. Plus it doesn't help that the gun was found in the victim's hand.

"If you don't need me anymore," she says, "I'd like to

leave?" Damn. She can't leave yet. She can't get away! Wait a second. I might have an idea. I run to the body and look at the key that was found on the body. I look closely and see a piece of tape on the key. I tell the other officers to search all the trashcans and wastebaskets in the house. Later they return with what I was looking for, a long piece of string. I walk up to the daughter. I invite her into the room where the crime happened.

"Would you like a pair of gloves?" I asked.

"No. I hate wearing gloves."

I smile and then walk away from her.

"Man, have you ever head of the 'Sealed Door trick?'"

She looks at me straight in the eye and says, "No."

"Then let me explain," I said, "It's a trick that most people have forgotten, since most doors today don't need a key to lock. With a door that can be locked only from the inside with a key, someone can easily give the illusion that the person in the room locked the door. All you need is a needle, string and some tape."

"How so?" she says.

"First you tape the string to the key. Then you lock the door, keeping the key in the door. Afterwards you move the string across the door and with the needle, loop the string in someone's pocket, by using the needle to poke through the pocket and keep stringing along until you make it to the door again. Next close the door with the string showing from underneath the door. We now have a locked door with no way of you getting in. You then pull on the string from underneath the door, making the key fall out of the lock and having it being strung across the room until it goes into the victim's pocket. You then give a good tug, in which you free the string, leaving the key in the victim's pocket, giving the illusion that they had it the whole time."

She stares blankly at me and says, "My, that's quite a trick."

"It is, considering that is what you did after you shot your father."

"Detective, I did not kill my father! Even if I did, you have no proof!"

"Miss," I said with a smile, "The tape will have your fingerprints on it." She looks at me in fear as I begin to approach her.

"It's a shame you hate wearing gloves."

She continues to look at me, like a deer caught in the headlights when I come up to her face to face.

"When I check that piece of tape, even if it's a partial, whose fingerprints will I find?" She looks away in shame as she brings her hands up and holds her arms.

"Whose fingerprints will I find?"

"Mine," she finally says.

"Thank you for your honesty," I say as I look up at my men, "Take her away and read her, her rights."

莫名其妙的伏击

[美国] 安布罗斯·比尔斯

连接里德维尔和伍德伯里之间的是一条长 9 到 10 英里的艰难的收费公路，道路崎岖不平。里德维尔是联邦军队在穆尔弗里斯伯勒的前哨站，伍德伯里与图拉荷马的联邦军队有着同样的关系。在斯通河大战之后的几个月里，这些前哨一直在争吵，大部分麻烦便发生在上文提到的收费公路上，在骑兵分遣队之间。有时，步兵和炮兵为了表现出他们的善意，也会参加战斗。

一天晚上，一个由机智勇敢的军官塞德尔少校指挥的联邦骑兵中队从里德维尔出发，执行一项危险的任务，需要保密，保持沉默，小心谨慎。

经过步兵纠察队后，分遣队很快就接近了两个骑兵哨兵，他们凝视着黑暗的前方。应该有三个骑马的哨兵。

"你们的另一个骑兵在哪里？"少校问道。"我命令邓宁今晚到这里来。"

"他骑马向前走了，长官。"那人回答。"后来发生了一点枪击，但离前线很远。"

"邓宁这么做是违反命令的，也是缺乏判断力的表现。"军官说，显然很生气。"他为什么向前骑?"

"不知道,先生,他好像特别焦躁不安。我猜他是害怕了。"

当这位杰出的推理家和他的同伴被远征军收编以后,队伍又继续前进了。禁止谈话;武器和装备被剥夺了喋喋不休的权力。听到的只有马匹的踩踏声,而且为了尽可能减弱踩踏声,行进缓慢。当时已经过了午夜,天很黑,尽管在云团后面的某个地方月亮露出了个头。

沿路走了两到三英里,纵队的队首接近一片茂密的雪松林,两边都与公路接壤。少校不自觉地停了下来,显然他自己有点"害怕",便独自骑着马去侦察。然而,他的副官和三名士兵跟在他的后面不远处,在他看不见的情况下看到了一切。

少校骑马向森林走了 100 码后,突然勒住马,坐在马鞍上纹丝不动。在路边附近一个小小的空地上,不到十步远的地方,站着一个像他一样纹丝不动的人,隐约可见。少校的第一感觉就是他对把骑兵留在后面感到很满意;如果这是一个敌人,就应该逃走,他就没有什么可报告的了。探险队还没有被发现。

在那人的脚边,有一个黑乎乎的东西依稀可辨,少校看不出来是什么。他凭借一个骑兵的本能,因为特别不愿意开枪,所以拔出了马刀。这个徒步的人对挑战没有任何反应。形势紧张,有点戏剧性。突然,月亮从云缝里钻了出来,在一片高大橡树的阴影下,在一片白月光下,骑手清晰地看见了那个徒步的人。那是没拿武器也没戴头盔的骑兵邓宁。他脚下的那个物体分解成了一匹死马,在马脖子上的一个直角处躺着一个死人,脸朝上躺在月光下。

"邓宁一生都在战斗。"少校想,正要向前冲去。邓宁举起手,示意他回来,做了个警告的手势;然后,他放下手臂,指着在雪松林的黑暗中迷失的路。

少校明白了,就把马转过来回到跟在他后面的那组人中。那组人因为怕他不高兴,已经走到后面去了,于是他再次回到了指挥岗位。

"邓宁就在前面。"他对带领着那个连队的上尉说。"他杀了自己人,另外还有一些情况要报告。"

他们耐心地等待着,拔出了马刀,但邓宁没有来。一个小时后,天色破晓,整个部队都小心翼翼地向前行进,指挥官对他私下派遣邓宁的信念并不完全满意。探险失败了,但还有一些事情要做。

在路边的空地上,他们发现了那匹倒下的马。以一个直角穿过马的脖子,脸朝上,一颗子弹射入大脑。骑兵邓宁的尸体躺在那里,僵硬得像一尊雕像,已经死了几个小时了。

调查显示,大量证据表明,半小时之内,雪松林就被一支强大的南方联邦步兵所占领——这是一场伏击。

A Baffled Ambuscade

By Ambrose Bierce

Connecting Readyville and Woodbury was a good, hard turnpike nine or ten miles long. Readyville was an outpost of the Federal army at Murfreesboro; Woodbury had the same relation to the Confederate army at Tullahoma. For months after the big battle at Stone River these outposts were in constant quarrel, most of the trouble occurring, naturally, on the turnpike mentioned, between detachments of cavalry. Sometimes the infantry and artillery took a hand in the game by way of showing their goodwill.

One night a squadron of Federal horse commanded by Major Seidel, a gallant and skillful officer, moved out from Readyville on an uncommonly hazardous enterprise requiring secrecy, caution and silence.

Passing the infantry pickets, the detachment soon afterward approached two cavalry videttes staring hard into the darkness ahead. There should have been three.

"Where is your other man?" said the major. "I ordered

Dunning to be here tonight."

"He rode forward, sir," the man replied. "There was a little firing afterward, but it was a long way to the front."

"It was against orders and against sense for Dunning to do that," said the officer, obviously vexed. "Why did he ride forward?"

"Don't know, sir; he seemed mighty restless. Guess he was skeered."

When this remarkable reasoner and his companion had been absorbed into the expeditionary force, it resumed its advance. Conversation was forbidden; arms and accoutrements were denied the right to rattle. The horses tramping was all that could be heard and the movement was slow in order to have as little as possible of that. It was after midnight and pretty dark, although there was a bit of moon somewhere behind the masses of cloud.

Two or three miles along, the head of the column approached a dense forest of cedars bordering the road on both sides. The major commanded a halt by merely halting, and, evidently himself a bit "skeered", rode on alone to reconnoiter. He was followed, however, by his adjutant and three troopers, who remained a little distance behind and, unseen by him, saw all that occurred.

After riding about a hundred yards toward the forest, the major suddenly and sharply reined in his horse and sat motionless in the saddle. Near the side of the road, in a little open space and hardly ten paces away, stood the figure of a man, dimly visible and as motionless as he. The major's first feeling was that of satisfaction in having left his cavalcade behind; if this were an enemy and should escape he would have little to report. The expedition was as yet undetected.

Some dark object was dimly discernible at the man's feet; the officer could not make it out. With the instinct of the true cavalryman and a particular indisposition to the discharge of firearms, he drew his saber. The man on foot made no movement in answer to the challenge. The situation was tense and a bit dramatic. Suddenly the moon burst through a rift in the clouds and, himself in the shadow of a group of great oaks, the horseman saw the footman clearly, in a patch of white light. It was Trooper Dunning, unarmed and bareheaded. The object at his feet resolved itself into a dead horse, and at a right angle across the animal's neck lay a dead man, face upward in the moonlight.

"Dunning has had the fight of his life," thought the major, and was about to ride forward. Dunning raised his hand, motioning him back with a gesture of warning; then, lowering the arm, he pointed to the place where the road lost itself in the blackness of the cedar forest.

The major understood, and turning his horse rode back to the little group that had followed him and was already moving to the rear in fear of his displeasure, and so returned to the head of his command.

"Dunning is just ahead there," he said to the captain of his leading company. "He has killed his man and will have something to report."

Right patiently they waited, sabers drawn, but Dunning did not come. In an hour the day broke and the whole force moved cautiously forward, its commander not altogether satisfied with his faith in Private Dunning. The expedition had failed, but something remained to be done.

In the little open space off the road they found the fallen horse. At a right angle across the animal's neck face upward, a bullet in the brain, lay the body of Trooper Dunning, stiff as a statue, hours dead.

Examination disclosed abundant evidence that within a half hour the cedar forest had been occupied by a strong force of Confederate infantry—an ambuscade.

化装舞会

拉切尔和摩西·科恩应邀参加一个要求戴华丽面具的光明节化装舞会,不巧的是,临出门前,拉切尔突然感觉头痛得厉害,便让摩西自己一个人去。作为一位忠诚的丈夫,摩西坚决反对。拉切尔劝慰丈夫说她吃点阿司匹林躺床上休息休息就好了,不要因为她不去而毁了他的快乐时光。摩西听她这么一说,也就换上化装舞会服、戴上面具去参加舞会了。

拉切尔吃了药,熟睡了一个多小时,然后醒了过来,感觉头一点儿也不疼了,看看时间还早,于是决定去参加舞会。她知道摩西不知道她准备穿什么样的化装舞会服装(话又说回来,又有几个丈夫能知道这些?),她想看看她不跟他在一起时他是什么表现,这一定很好玩。就这样,拉切尔穿上化装舞会服装,开着车来到开舞会的地方。

很快,拉切尔看到了摩西。摩西正在舞场上鬼混,尽可能地与每一个女子跳舞,东摸一把,西吻一下。于是拉切尔悄悄走到他身边,搔首弄姿,大秀性感。摩西立刻就被她吸引,把所有的时间都花到她的身上——花在她这位刚刚到达的新的美女身上。

拉切尔让他为所欲为,这很自然,毕竟他是她丈夫。所以,当他在耳边说出一个小小的提议时,她同意了。他们去了一个停车场,疯狂地激情做爱。

午夜前夕,当聚会上的所有人都必须脱下化装舞会服装的时候,拉切尔偷偷溜了出来回了家,藏好了化装舞会的服装和面具,上了床,她要看看摩西回来怎么解释他的所作所为。

摩西进屋时,拉切尔正坐着看书,她问他玩得开不开心。

"唉,都是老样子。你又不是不知道,你不在的话,我玩得都不开心。"

她问:"你舞跳得尽兴吧?"

他答道:"拉切尔,我告诉你,我一支舞也没跳。我一到聚会上,就遇到了约什、罗伯特、大卫,还有其他朋友,我们便找了个后屋打了一晚上的牌。不过,我可以告诉你,拉切尔,向我借化装舞会服装的那个家伙好像玩得特别开心!"

The Chanukah Party

Rachel and Moshe Cohen were invited to a posh masked, fancy dress Chanukah party. Unfortunately, Rachel got a terrible headache and told Moshe to go to the party alone. Being a devoted husband, Moshe protested, but she argued and said she was going to take some aspirin and go to bed and there was no need of his good time being spoiled by not going. So Moshe put on his costume and mask and away he went to the party.

After sleeping soundly for an hour or so, Rachel awoke without pain and as it was still early, decided to go to the party. She knew that Moshe didn't know what costume she was going to wear (how many husbands do?) and she thought she would have some fun by watching him to see how he acts when she was not with him. So Rachel put on her costume and mask and drove off to the party.

Rachel soon spotted Moshe. He was fooling around on the dance floor, dancing with every girl he could, copping a little feel here and having a little kiss there. So Rachel sidled up to him and being a rather seductive lady, Moshe immediately left his partner and devoted all his time to her—to the new beauty that had just arrived.

Rachel let him go as far as he wished; naturally, since he was her husband. So when he whispered a little proposition in her ear, she agreed. Off they went to one of the parked cars and made mad, passionate love.

Just before midnight, when everyone at the party had to take off their masks, Rachel slipped away, went home, put her costume away, got into bed, and wondered what kind of explanation Moshe would make for his behaviour.

Rachel was sitting up reading when Moshe came in and she asked what kind of time he had.

He said, "Oh, the same old thing. You know I never have a good time when you're not there."

Then she asked, "Did you dance much?"

He replied, "I'll tell you, Rachel, I never even danced one dance. When I got to the party, I bumped into Yossi, Roberto, David and some other guys, so we went into a back room and played cards all night. But I can tell you, Rachel, the guy I loaned my costume to sure had a real good time!"

黑暗之屋

[尼泊尔] 迪佩什·奥哈

乔西先生在电影院看完电影准备回家。此时是晚上 10 点钟,夜场电影早结束了一个小时。

乔西先生心情非常好。因为电影很有意思,男主角虽然是个新闻工作者,却单枪匹马就干掉了所有坏人,乔西很喜欢这个片段。就像大部分尼泊尔电影一样,这部电影也是个大团圆结局。男主角不仅得到了女主角的青睐,还赢得了女主角父母的欢心,让女主角嫁给他。电影的最后一个镜头是男女主角互吻,看着这一幕,观众都欢呼,吹口哨,鼓掌喝彩。

他经常独自一人去看电影,都不记得上次是什么时候带太太乔西去电影院或者其他地方了。在家里,他们有自己的私人小生活,尊重彼此的隐私。在跟他结婚之前,乔西太太是一个寡妇。他本来不打算结婚,但最后还是顺从了家人的意愿,决定在 38 岁时结婚。回家时要路过一条从大路岔开的小路。小路的一边是几块菜地,种着圆白菜、小萝卜、水萝卜。晚上走这条路有点费劲。他用袖珍手电照明,手电发出了一束稳定的光。

他快到自家二层楼附近的时候,听到家里的番石榴树树叶沙沙作响。他拿手电往那边一照,看到了一个人的轮廓站在树下。不过不应该说是一个人。

轮廓中只有人的身体部分,穿着黑色西装。只有脖子以下具备人类的特征,因为没有头。

乔西失声尖叫,扔掉手电筒,往后倒了下去。手电筒掉在地上,闪了一秒钟,最后还是照着草地。乔西太太肯定没有听见他的尖叫,如果听见他像疯子一样在门口尖叫,她就会到阳台看看的。

他爬起身,跌跌撞撞地往门口跑。他用拳头砸门。在他不停砸门的时候,他还能看到那具身体还在原来的位置。它尴尬地立在那里,就好像脖子上吊着一根绳子似的。然后,它死气沉沉地抽搐了一下。

终于,他听见屋里传来了脚步声,门开了。他猛地冲到屋子里,撞到了太太身上,还差点儿摔倒在地板上。

"你要干什——"乔西太太开口道。

"外面!"他说。他害怕得几乎要说不出话了。"在外面!"他指着门大喊。他现在只能说这么多了。

乔西太太走出门外,看了看,回头喊道:"这里什么也没有。"

"有一个——一个人,一个没有身体的人!"他本来想说"一个没有头的人"。他气喘吁吁得像一个溺水的人。

乔西太太关上门,看着他,一脸的困惑。

"你在沙发上坐一下,你现在需要一杯热茶。"说着,她朝厨房走去。

"等等!"他还在瑟瑟发抖,挣扎着要说出连贯的句子。"我跟你一块儿去!"他脱口而出。

她对他微微一笑,走向厨房,他跟在后面。

当乔西看见一具穿着黑色西装、没有头的身体坐在餐桌前的时候,他发出了一声让人毛骨悚然的尖叫声。它站了起来。

他吓得魂飞魄散，转身去看他的太太，想一把抓住她，带上她跑出去。但是，他却看到她手上拿着一把刀，脸上挂着一抹邪恶的笑……

接下来，灯灭了……

House of Darkness

By Deepesh Ojha

Mr. Joshi was on his way back home from the cinema. It was 10 P.M. and the evening show had finished just an hour earlier.

He was in a happy mood. The movie had been interesting—he liked the part where the hero fought and defeated all the villains single-handedly despite his background in journalism. Like most Nepali movies it had a happy ending and the hero not only managed to get the girl but also was able to convince the girl's parents to let him marry her. The audience had cheered and whistled and applauded when the couple finally kissed and then the movie ended.

He used to go to the cinema alone. He could not remember the last time he took Mrs. Joshi to the cinema or anywhere else. Inside their house, they had their own private little lives and each respected the other's privacy. Mrs. Joshi had been a widow before he married her. He had decided to stay unmarried until he finally yielded to his family's wishes and decided to marry at the age of thirty-eight. There was a narrow path that branched out from the main road that led to his house. On either side of the path there were vegetable patches—cabbages, little radishes and turnips. It was difficult to navigate the path at night. His pocket torchlight lit the way, projecting a consistent beam of light.

As he approached his two-storied house he heard the sound of leaves rustling in the direction of his guava trees. As he pointed his torch in that direction he saw a silhouette of a man standing just below the trees. Except it wasn't a man.

It had the body of a man—in a black suit. His humanlike qualities ended just as the neck began. It was a headless body.

Mr. Joshi let out a scream. He dropped his torch and fell back. The torch fell on the ground and flickered for a second but continued illuminating the grass. Mrs. Joshi must have not heard his scream; she would have come outside the verandah if she had heard him screaming in front of the house like a lunatic.

He picked himself up and stumbled towards the door. He banged the door with his fists. As he banged the door incessantly, he could see the body at the same place where he had first seen it. It was standing awkwardly—as if it was hung by the neck with a rope. Then it gave a lifeless twitch.

Finally, he heard footsteps from inside and the door opened and he burst inside. He bumped into his wife and nearly fell on the floor.

"What are you d—" she began.

"Out!" He said. He could not speak. "Outside!" he cried as he pointed to the door. It was all he could say.

She went outside. "There is nothing out here." she called back.

"A m-man" he stuttered "A man with no body!" He wanted to say "a man with no head". He was breathing like of a drowning man.

Mrs. Joshi closed the door and looked at him with a perplexed expression.

"Just sit there on the sofa. What you need is a warm cup of tea." she said as she started walking towards the kitchen.

"Wait!" he said still shaking violently and struggling to from coherent sentences. "I'll come with you!" he blurted out.

She gave him a smile and went to the kitchen and he straggled behind her.

He let out a bloodcurdling scream as he saw the body—sitting on the dining table—black suited and headless. It got up.

Horrified, he turned towards his wife to grab her and get out of the house. Instead, he saw a knife in her hand and a wicked smile on her face…

And then the lights went out.

河狸传奇

[美国]詹姆斯·珀灵

河狸们在缅因州汉普登镇安家落户的时候,人们还不太知道如何处理水坝隐患。但是,根据镇长莱斯里·斯坦利的看法,近期形势看起来不会有改观。他说:"我们遇到的问题确实很棘手。"

5月底,棘手的问题出现了。在镇外大约3英里远的迦南公路附近,有一条排放溪水的排水渠,一群河狸在排泄口附近修建了一座水坝。水坝堵塞了流水,排水渠漫出的水淹没了两侧约50英尺的公路和几百英尺的田地。斯坦利派出一支养路队,去夷平那座水坝。河狸们重建了水坝。养路队又把水坝豁开。实际上,他们连续10天在早晨都把水坝豁开,而河狸立刻在这10天的夜里重建了水坝。

在第11天,养路队的队长狠狠地咒骂着,把难题踢给了镇长。镇长反过来又踢给了当地的狩猎警察。这位警察熟知河狸习性,在一天夜里悄悄溜过去,在水坝上罩了一个浸透汽油的麻布口袋(河狸专家都知道,这种动物根本无法忍受汽油的味道)。

早晨,人们发现口袋被巧妙地编进了水坝。

那天夜里,警察设置了三架钢制捕捉器。到了早晨,一个捕捉器是空的,另外两个被河狸偷走,用于支撑水坝。警察咒骂州法律不准用火器猎取河狸,只好收回捕捉器,再重置。他重置了一次一次又一次……可是,每天夜里河狸都把捕捉器偷走。

斯坦利镇长征召队伍。他给警察局长打电话。那些河狸违反了州里有关阻碍自然水道的法律。"为什么你不去维护这项法律呢?"斯坦利问道。"你是警察局长,应该驱逐它们,剥夺它们的权利,逮捕它们。采取措施啊!"

过了三个上午,警察局长骄傲地宣称水坝被平了。他说,凌晨两点钟,他和一名持证的爆破员已经把水坝炸得粉碎。斯坦利说要眼见为实。

他们驱车赶往排水渠,发现一道新的水坝已经建成了一半。他们还发现,炸药抛起的泥浆和碎屑阻塞了公路,动用了四名消防员和消防局的500加仑抽水车,还有三个警察,花费了一个半小时用水管才把这些垃圾冲刷干净。

斯坦利说,或许他们应该召集工程兵部队。但是,警察局长坚定不移地相信炸药。他发起了全面进攻。时间从6月进入7月,一夜又一夜,爆破的声音破坏了夏夜的空气——用小剂量炸药在水坝上撕开口子,不让水坝完整地得见天日。等负责扫尾工程的消防队员清晨出现在现场时,河狸们总是设法把炸开的洞堵上。

终于,河狸们厌倦了这种胡闹行为,把它们的水坝搬到了排水渠"内部"——要是在这里爆破水坝,势必要破坏公路。

斯坦利和手下的参谋部人员开了一个紧急军事会议,大家达成要实施的新战略。随后,他们灵机一动有了主意。他们的推理是:假如我们用人工拆走水坝的每一根树枝,我们就是在强迫河狸去寻找新的建筑材料,代替我们运走的树枝。然后,我们可以沿着它们的河道放置陷笼,把它们捕获——可能吧。

全体人员一致通过了这个计划。不仅如此,这项行动还卓有成效。7月30日,斯坦利镇长宣布:河狸群已经被捕获并移送到偏远的荒郊野外。汉普登镇上一片欢腾——一直持续到10月中旬,有人看到一群年幼的河狸在水域里游泳,而这正是近期捕获老河狸的那片水域。

长话短说,人们也对年幼的河狸实施了对老河狸行之有效的措施。

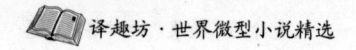

A Beaver Anecdote

By James Poling

They don't quite know how to cope with all the dam trouble they've got down in Hampden, Maine. And according to town manager Leslie Stanley, it doesn't look as if things will improve any in the immediate future. "We've got a real gnawing problem on our hands," he says.

The gnawing began in late May. About three miles outside of town a colony of beavers built a dam near the mouth of a culvert that carries a stream under Canaan Road. Some 50 feet of roadway and several hundred feet of land on each side of the culvert were flooded. Stanley sent a road crew out to level the dam. The beavers rebuilt it. The crew tore it apart again. In fact, they tore it apart for ten mornings in a row—and for ten straight nights the beavers rebuilt it.

On the eleventh day, the foreman of the crew said to-hell-with-it and tossed the problem back to the town manager. He, in turn, tossed it on to the local game warden. The warden, steeped in beaver lore, crept out one night and draped a gasoline-soaked burlap bag over the dam. (Any beaver expert will tell you the creatures just can't abide gasoline fumes.)

In the morning the bag was found artistically woven into the dam.

The warden set out three steel traps that night. In the morning one was empty. The other two had been stolen by the beavers and used to buttress the dam. The warden, cursing the state law against hunting beavers with firearms, got his traps back and set them out again...and again...and again...And every night the beavers stole them.

Town manager Stanley enlisted additional troops. He telephoned his police chief. Those beavers were breaking a state law against blocking up a natural watercourse. "Why aren't you out there upholding the law?" Stanley asked. "You're the police chief. So evict 'em. Dispossess them. Arrest them. Do something."

Three mornings later, the police chief proudly announced the end of the dam. At 2:00 A.M., he said, he and a licensed dynamiter had blown it to smithereens. Stanley said he'd believe it when he saw it.

They drove out to the culvert and found a new dam already half-built. They also found the highway so choked with mud and debris thrown up by the dynamite that it took four firemen, the fire department's 500-gallon pumper, and three constables an hour and a half to hose away the mess.

Stanley said maybe they should call in the Army Corps of

Engineers. But the police chief's faith in explosives was unshaken. He launched an all-out campaign. Night after night, as June drifted into July, the sound of blasting shattered the summer air—and tore holes in the dam that never saw the full light of day. The beavers always managed to have the holes plugged by the time the fire department appeared on the scene for its morning mop-up.

In time, the beavers tired of this nonsense and moved their dam "inside" the culvert—where it couldn't be blown up without destroying the road too.

Stanley and his general staff held a council of war and agreed that fresh strategy was called for. Then they came up with an inspired idea. If we remove every branch of the dam by hand, they reasoned, we'll force the beavers to go in search of new building material to replace what we've taken. Then we can place box traps along their runways and capture them—maybe.

The plan was unanimously approved. Moreover it worked. On July 30, town manager Stanley was able to announce that the beaver colony had been trapped and removed to a remote wilderness area. And there was great rejoicing in Hampden—until the middle of October, that is, when a colony of young beavers was spotted swimming in the same waters from which its elders had recently been snatched.

But to make a long story short, the strategy that worked with the older beavers worked with the young ones too.

我从来不吃比萨

[美国]索尔·格林布拉特

亚当·卡尔和菲尔·邓恩都是物理学家,他们正在大学自助餐厅里的一张桌子上吃午饭。亚当一边吃汉堡一边听菲尔说话。"亚当,著名物理学家都相信会有很多平行世界,世界上有别的亚当·卡尔们。"

"他们相信什么和他们能证明什么是两码事。我认为他们的想象力只有在梦里才能得到发挥。这不过是痴心妄想罢了。"

"亚当,你是一名科学家。作为一名科学家,你就不能接受存在平行宇宙的理念吗?"

"我是一名用事实讲话的科学家。我相信眼见为实。"

"好吧,我可以凭直觉感觉到平行世界的存在。说到底,为什么不能存在呢?"菲尔说着看了看表。"该去上课了,我们以后再谈。再见……在另一个世界。"他轻轻地笑着离开了。

那天晚上,亚当一直在批改试卷,感觉累了以后便停了下来。"剩下的我明天早上接着改。"他说着就上床睡觉了。早上,他去书房批改试卷。当他开始工作时,房间里的灯熄灭了,房间笼罩在黑暗中。"该死。我什么也看不见了,我的手电筒在哪里?"他咕哝着,在房间里跌跌撞撞地走着,并打开了灯。"嗯?那是……"他边说边呆住了。

"我的桌子在房间的另一边,这是不可能的。屋里的东西都挪了地方:椅子、灯、沙发。这不可能,但是……到底发生了什么?我疯了吗?我怎么了?"他说着,浑身颤抖。"我需要一杯烈酒冷静一下。"他说着,急忙跑到厨房。他在厨房橱柜里放了一瓶威士忌。"什么……厨房在哪里?这是洗衣房。"

"厨房在哪里?"他说着,匆匆走出洗衣房进了另一个房间。"厨房怎么在这里?在这里的应该是餐厅。天哪,我疯了。什么都不在应该在的地方了。"他擦着额头的汗说。"上帝,帮帮我。"他抬起头来恳求道。

"我必须离开这里。"他低声说着跑向他的车,开车去了大学。停车后,他慢慢地走向科学楼,一边走一边咕哝。"我得去教物理课。我都疯了,怎么能集中精力教物理呢?"他说着就去了教室。"这里没人。"他说,声音听起来很困惑。他走进大厅,看见一个学生朝他跑来。

"卡尔教授,全班都在等你。"

"他们在等我吗?他们都在哪儿?"

"在我们以前上课的地方啊。103教室。"

"我们不是在109教室上课吗?"

"不是,"她咯咯地笑着,"那是上语言学的教室。"

"语言学,对,语言学。好的,我们赶紧去吧。"

下课后,他向自助餐厅冲去。"我得告诉菲尔。"当他走进自助餐厅时,他倒抽了一口冷气。"我疯了。全都不一样了,所有的东西都不在原位了。"他环顾四周,听到菲尔在叫他。"菲尔在另一张桌子。"他咕哝着走到那张桌子前。

"很高兴你在这里。我怕你来晚了,就给你点了你最喜欢的午餐:意大利辣香肠蘑菇比萨。祝你好胃口。"

"比萨？我从来不吃比萨啊。"他盯着比萨心中暗想。

"菲尔，我午餐吃过汉堡吗？"

"汉堡？"他轻笑道，"你不喜欢汉堡啊。"

"菲尔，你怎么了？我喜欢吃汉堡，讨厌吃比萨。你听见我说话了吗？我从来不吃比萨。"他咆哮着，跳了起来，用拳头捶着桌子。"我从来不吃比萨。"

"菲尔·邓恩是知道这一点的。你不是菲尔。你是谁？"他大叫着，环顾四周一会儿，然后跑出自助餐厅，沿着走廊跑下去。"他们是对的，还有其他平行世界。"他靠在墙上喘着气说，"我的世界在哪里？我的办公桌应该在原处的那个世界在哪里？那个我吃汉堡的世界在哪里？我必须找到我的世界。"

"无论我现在在哪里，我都不属于这里。我必须在疯掉之前找到我的世界。"他咆哮着，开始深呼吸。这时，所有的灯灭了一会儿。当灯再次亮起来时，另一个亚当·卡尔正和另一个菲尔·邓恩坐在自助餐厅的桌子旁。亚当一边听菲尔说话，一边享受着他的比萨。"亚当，著名的物理学家会相信有很多的平行世界，世界上有别的亚当·卡尔们。"

"亚当，你是一名科学家。作为一名科学家，你就不能接受平行宇宙存在的理念吗？"

"我是一名用事实讲话的科学家。我相信眼见为实。他们相信什么和他们能证明什么是两码事。我认为他们的想象力只有在梦里才能得到发挥。这不过是痴心妄想罢了。"

"好吧，我凭直觉感觉平行世界是存在的。说到底，为什么不能存在呢？"菲尔说着看了看表。"该去上课了，我们以后再谈。等会儿见……在另一个世界。"他轻声笑着，留下亚当一个人继续吃比萨。

I Never Eat Pizza

By Saul Greenblatt

Adam Carr and Phil Dunn, both physicists, sat at a table in the university cafeteria eating lunch. Adam enjoyed a hamburger while listening to Phil. "Adam, reputable physicists believe that there are many parallel worlds, worlds where there are other Adam Carrs."

"What they believe and what they can prove are two different things. I think their imaginations are looking for something to dream about. Wishful thinking, that's all."

"Adam, you're a scientist. As a scientist, can't you even entertain the idea that there are parallel universes?"

"I am one scientist who deals with facts. I'll believe it when I see it."

"Well, I feel in my bones that there are parallel worlds. After all, why not?" Phil said and looked at his watch. "Time to go to class. We'll talk some more. See you later…in another world," he chuckled and left.

That night, Adam corrected exams until he got tired. "I'll

correct the rest in the morning," he said and went to bed. In the morning, he went to his den to correct the exams. As he worked, the lights in his den went out and the room became shrouded in darkness. "Damn. I can't see a thing. Where is my flashlight?" he mumbled, and, as he stumbled around the room, the lights went on. "Well, that's…" he said and froze.

"My desk is on the other side of the room. That's impossible. Everything is in a different place. The chairs. The lamps. The couch. This is impossible, but…what the hell is going on? Have I lost my mind? What's happening to me?" he said, shaking. "I need a stiff drink to calm me down," he said and hurried to the kitchen where he kept a bottle of whiskey in a cabinet. "What the…where's the kitchen? This is the laundry room."

"Where's the kitchen?" he said and hurried out of the laundry room into another room. "What's the kitchen doing here? The dining room is supposed to be here. God, I am losing my mind. Nothing is where it's suppose to be," he said wiping his brow. "God, help me," he pleaded looking up.

"I have to get out of here," he whispered and ran to his car, and drove to the university. After he parked, he walked slowly to the science building, mumbling as he walked. "I have to teach my physics class. How will I be able to concentrate on physics when I'm losing my mind," he said and went to his classroom. "Nobody's here," he said sounding confused, went into the hall and saw a student running toward him.

"Dr. Carr. The class is waiting for you."

"They're waiting? Uh, where are they?"

"Where we always have class. In room 103."

"We don't have class in 109?"

"No," she giggled. "That room is for the linguistics class."

"Linguistics, of course, linguistics. Okay, let's go."

After his class, he rushed to the cafeteria. "I have to tell Phil." When he entered the cafeteria, he gasped. "I have lost my mind. It's different. Everything is in different places." As he looked around, he heard Phil call him. "Phil is at another table," he mumbled and went to the table.

"Glad you're here. I ordered your favorite lunch just in case you were going to be late. Pizza with pepperoni and mushrooms. Bon appetite."

"Pizza? I never eat pizza," he thought staring at the pizza.

"Phil, did I ever eat hamburgers for lunch?"

"Hamburgers," he chuckled. "You don't like hamburgers."

"Phil, what's wrong with you? I love hamburgers. I hate pizza. Do you hear me? I never eat pizza," he growled, jumped up and pounded the table with his fist: "I never eat pizza."

"Phil Dunn knows that. You're not Phil. Who are you?" he yelled, looked around for a moment and then ran out of the cafeteria and ran down a corridor. "They're right. There are other worlds," he said gasping and leaned against a wall. "Where is my world? The world where my desk is where it's supposed to be. The world where I eat hamburgers. I have to find my world."

"Wherever I am, I don't belong here. I have to find my world before I go mad," he growled and took deep breaths. As he did, the lights went out for a few moments. When they came on, another Adam Carr was sitting at a table in the cafeteria with another Phil Dunn. Adam enjoyed his pizza while he listened to Phil. "Adam, reputable physicists believe that there are many parallel worlds, worlds where there are other Adam Carrs."

"Adam, you're a scientist. As a scientist, can't you even entertain the idea that there might be parallel universes?"

"I am one scientist who deals with facts. I'll believe it when I see it. What they believe and what they can prove are two different things. I think their imaginations are looking for something to dream about. Wishful thinking, that's all."

"Well, I feel in my bones that there are parallel worlds. After all, why not?" Phil said and looked at his watch. "Time to go to class. We'll talk some more. See you later…in another world," he chuckled and left leaving Adam to finish his pizza.

炸弹惊魂

[美国] 比尔·普洛奇尼

他此时情绪高度紧张。这个小个子长着布雷尔兔似的大耳朵和大龅牙，穿着破旧的褐色外衣，戴着太阳眼镜。他左手提的公文包一根带子断了，由一根磨破的皮带勾着，看上去好像随时会崩开似的。公文包里面是……

"炸弹！"他用尖厉的声音一次次宣布，"这是遥控炸弹。照我说的做，不要过来，不然我们都得完蛋！"

旧金山信托银行分行的人都离他远远的。经理劳伦斯·梅塔克萨和其他银行职员都在那排出纳柜台后面一动不动。包括我在内共四名顾客，都簇拥在前面，我们谁也不敢动弹，只能紧张地等着跳来跳去的"小兔子"开始干他的正事。

几秒钟以后，他才停下来。用那只空着的手从口袋里拽出一个布袋子扔给一名出纳。"把所有钱都装进去。离无声警铃远点儿，不然我就引爆炸弹。我说到做到！"

梅塔克萨声音颤抖着向他保证，他说什么，他们就做什么。

"那就快点儿！""兔子"挥着空着的右手，摇摇晃晃，好像在指挥某种疯狂的交响乐似的。"快！快！"

出纳们顿时忙了起来。当他们挨个儿腾空现金抽屉时,小个子又拿出一个布袋朝我走来。其他顾客吓得直往后退,只有我站在原地不动,于是他把袋子扔给我。

"把你的钱包放进去,"他的声音像玻璃破碎的声音,"把你所有值钱的东西都放进去。然后再去收其他人的!"

我说:"不行。"

"什么?什么?"他一只脚跳起来,然后另一只脚也跳了一下,公文包也随着跳了起来。"你说什么?照我说的做!"

他刚进来的时候就开始嚷嚷着身上有炸弹,我还以为自己选了一个最糟糕的时间点来存钱呢。现在我想的是,我再也选不出比这更好的时间了。我从容不迫地往前迈了一步。后面的人倒吸了一口凉气。我又向前迈了一步。

"别过来!"小个子喊道,"不然我就按下按钮,我会把大家都炸死。"

"不,你不能。"我说着冲向他并夺过了他手里的公文包。

更多气喘吁吁的声音出现,还有人大喊了一声,以及顾客和职员争着抢着找掩体的声音。但什么都没发生,只有小个子试图逃跑。我一把抓住他的衣领,把他拽回来。他挣扎了几下,动作很敷衍。他被我抓住的时候就知道自己赌输了。

从柜台里面、角落里露出了一张张惊恐万状的脸。我把公文包举得高高的,让他们都看得清楚。"这儿没炸弹,朋友们,你们可以放松了,都结束了。"

过了两分钟才渐渐恢复了秩序,在此期间,我把小个子押到梅塔克萨的办公桌前,把他按在椅子上。他颓唐地坐在那里,身体抽搐着,嘴里喃喃自语:"工作丢了,还有那么多债……我一定是疯了才来抢银行……我很难过，对不起。"可怜的"小兔子"，让他更难过的还在后面呢。

梅塔克萨报警的时候我打开了公文包。里面只有一本城市电话簿，用来压重。

梅塔克萨挂断电话以后，对我说："你刚才那样子抢公文包太疯狂，太冒险了。如果里面真的有炸弹……"

"我知道没有炸弹。"

"你知道？你怎么知道的？"

"我是个侦探，对吧？有三个理由。一、炸弹是很精巧的装置，造炸弹的人必定十分小心谨慎。他们不会把爆炸物放到坏了一根带子只用破皮带勾着的廉价包里，除非拿炸弹的人想自杀。二、他声称是遥控炸弹，但他那只不停挥舞着的手是空空的，他的全部装置都在另一只手拿着的包里。那么，遥控器在哪里？难道放在不方便拿的口袋里？不。真正有炸弹的人不会在众目睽睽之下拿着炸弹壮胆。"

"不过，"梅塔克萨说，"你还是有可能在这两点判断失误的。很难有绝对的把握。"

"是的，所以第三个理由最有把握。"

"什么？"

"制造炸弹不仅需要技术，还需要胆量、冷静、耐心，手也要稳。看看我们这位朋友。他一样都不占。他属于那种习惯性紧张的类型，猫似的跳来跳去。他是不可能造得出炸弹的，就像我和你不可能会飞一样。如果他尝试去造，不出两分钟，自己就会被炸飞。"

Bomb Scare

By Bill Pronzini

He was a hypertensive little man with overlarge ears and buck teeth—Brer Rabbit dressed up in a threadbare brown suit and sunglasses. In his left hand he carried a briefcase with a broken catch; it was held closed by a frayed strap that looked as though it might pop loose at any second. And inside the briefcase...

"A bomb," he kept announcing in a shrill voice. "I've got a remote-controlled bomb in here. Do what I tell you, don't come near me, or I'll blow us all up."

Nobody in the branch office of the San Francisco Trust Bank was anywhere near him. Lawrence Metaxa, the manager, and the other bank employees were frozen behind the row of tellers' cages. The four customers, me included, stood in a cluster out front. None of us was doing anything except waiting tensely for the little rabbit to quit hopping around and get down to business.

It took him another few seconds. Then, with his free hand, he dragged a cloth sack from his coat and threw it at one of the tellers.

"Put all the money in there. Stay away from the silent alarm or I'll set off the bomb. I mean it."

Metaxa assured him in a shaky voice that they would do whatever he asked.

"Hurry up, then." The rabbit waved his empty right hand in the air, jerkily, as if he were directing some sort of mad symphony. "Hurry up, hurry up!"

The tellers got busy. While they hurriedly emptied cashdrawers, the little man produced a second cloth sack and moved in my direction. The other customers shrank back. I stayed where I was, so he pitched the sack to me.

"Put your wallet in there," he said in a voice like glass cracking. "All your valuables. Then get everybody else's."

I said, "I don't think so."

"What? What?" He hopped on one foot, then the other, making the briefcase dance. "What's the matter with you? Do what I told you!"

When he'd first come in and started yelling about his bomb, I'd thought that I couldn't have picked a worse time to take care of my bank deposits. Now I was thinking that I couldn't have picked a better time. I took a measured step toward him. Somebody behind me gasped. I took another step.

"Stay back!" the little guy shouted. "I'll push the button, I'll blow us up."

I said, "No, you won't," and rushed him and yanked the briefcase out of his hand.

More gasps, a cry, the sounds of customers and employees scrambling for cover. But nothing happened, except that the little guy tried to run away. I caught him by the collar and dragged him back. His struggles were brief and half-hearted; he'd gambled and lost and he knew when he was licked.

Scared faces peered over counters and around corners. I held the briefcase up so they could all see it. "No bomb in here, folks. You can relax now, it's all over."

It took a couple of minutes to restore order, during which time I marched the little man around to Metaxa's desk and pushed him into a chair. He sat slumped, twitching and muttering. "Lost my job, so many debts…must've been crazy to do a thing like this…I'm sorry, I'm sorry." Poor little rabbit. He wasn't half as sorry now as he was going to be later.

I opened the case while Metaxa called the police. The only thing inside was a city telephone directory for weight.

When Metaxa hung up he said to me, "You took a crazy risk, grabbing the briefcase like that. If he really had had a bomb in there …"

"I knew he didn't."

"Knew he didn't? How could you?"

"I'm a detective, remember? Three reasons. One: Bombs are

delicate mechanisms and people who build them are cautious by necessity. They don't put explosives in a cheap case with a busted catch and just a frayed strap holding it together, not unless they're suicidal. Two: He claimed it was remote-controlled. But the hand he kept waving was empty and all he had in the other one was the case. Where was the remote control? In one of his pockets, where he couldn't get at it easily? No. A real bomber would've had it out in plain sight to back up his threat."

"Still," Metaxa said, "you could've been wrong on both counts. Neither is an absolute certainty."

"No, but the third reason is as close to one as you can get."

"Yes?"

"It takes more than just skill to make a bomb. It takes nerve, coolness, patience, and a very steady hand. Look at our friend here. He doesn't have any of those attributes; he's the chronically nervous type, as jumpy as six cats. He could no more manufacture an explosive device than you or I could fly. If he'd ever tried, he'd have blown himself up in two minutes flat."

一堆旧垃圾

[英国] 杰克·奥尔索普

达比小姐是那种从来不扔任何东西的人。"你永远不知道什么时候可能会用得着。"这是她最喜欢说的口头禅。她孤身一人住在我们对面一座维多利亚时期的大房子里。虽然我从未进去过,但我知道房子里装满了值钱的东西:古董家具、波斯地毯等。她热爱艺术;她家的墙上挂满了画。我记得我父亲说过她是"斯塔福德那达比"。当时我并不明白他的意思。多年后,我发现达比家族在斯塔福德那郡靠煤矿开采赚了钱。我们这些小孩过去常常编些关于她的故事。我的妹妹爱丽丝是一个浪漫主义者,对我们低声说:"她订过婚,但她的未婚夫在第一次世界大战中丧生了,所以现在她孤身一人伤心地生活。"

我的弟弟艾伦刚刚进入青春期,他另有想法:"他们说她是一个白女巫,只要盯着那些画看,就能治好脸上的斑点。"

凭借我狂野的想象力,我编造出自己关于达比小姐的故事:"她有六个孩子,她把他们锁在一个黑暗的地窖里。"

她很少出门,也没人去看望她。除了她的女管家特里格斯太太。特里格斯太太是我母亲的一个朋友,也是个长舌妇。有一天,我听她说达比小姐从来不扔任何东西。

"好多捆报纸！到处都是报纸！我想把它们扔掉，但是她会出去再把它们捡回来。我就放弃了！"

"再喝杯茶吧，特里格斯太太。"

直到她去世我们才发现达比小姐有两个侄子。他们继承了一切：她的钱、房子和里面的东西。侄子们过来跟我家打了声招呼，我妈妈给他们泡了茶。

"你们想搬进去住吗？"我妈妈彬彬有礼地问道。

"天哪，不！我们住在斯塔福德。不，我们只是来搬东西的。"

"我相信你们的姑姑有……曾经有许多好东西。"

侄子们点了点头。他们描述了房子里的情况。听起来就像是阿拉丁的洞穴。

接下来的几天里，我们这些孩子看着他们进进出出，希望我们也能加入他们的行列。大部分东西都被一辆大型家具货车运走了。他们也有一辆更小的货车，可以把姑姑不想处理的垃圾运走，大部分是大捆大捆的报纸。我的弟弟艾伦问侄子们是否可以给他一捆报纸。我们在报纸上看到一条头条新闻——"俄罗斯坦克开进布达佩斯"。日期是1956年11月10日！艾伦拿出他的袖珍折刀，割断了捆报纸的绳子。我们把报纸摊开，好奇地读着50年前发生的事情。

"这是什么？"爱丽丝问，手里拿着她在最上面的报纸里找到的东西。

"这里还有！"艾伦说着打开包裹里的第二份报纸。

"还有！还有！"我一边读着报纸一边喊道。

"那是些什么东西？看起来像是没有装裱的画。"

光是这一捆就有25幅美丽的画。后来我们得知，它们是真品，每幅至少值500英镑。当侄子们得知我们发现画的时候，他们已经把大部分的报纸都扔掉了。

A Load of Old Rubbish

By Jake Allsop

Miss Darby was one of those people who never threw anything away. "*You never know when you might need it,*" was one of her favourite sayings. She lived alone in a large Victorian house across the road from us. Although I never went into house, I knew it was full of valuable things: antique furniture, Persian carpets and so on. She loved art; every inch of her walls was taken up by paintings. I can remember my father saying that she was "a Staffordshire Darby". I have no idea what he meant. I found out years later that the Darby family had made their money from coalmining in the county of Staffordshire. We children used to make up stories about her. My sister Alice, who was a romantic, whispered to us: "She was engaged to be married, but her fiancé was killed in the Great War. Now she lives alone, broken-hearted."

My brother Alan, who was just coming into adolescence, had another idea: "They say she's a white witch and she can cure spots just staring at them."

With my wild imagination, I had my own story about Miss Darby: "She's got six children. She keeps them locked in a dark cellar."

She rarely went out, and nobody came to visit her. Nobody, that is, except for Mrs. Triggs, her housekeeper. Mrs. Triggs was a friend of my mother's and a great gossip. One day I heard her saying how Miss Darby never threw anything away.

"Bundles of newspapers! Hundreds of them, everywhere! I try to throw them out, but she just goes out and brings them back into the house. I give up!"

"Have another cup of tea, Mrs. Triggs."

It was only when she died that we found out that Miss Darby had two nephews. They inherited everything: her money, and the house and its contents. The nephews came across to say hello, and my mother made them a cup of tea.

"Are you thinking of moving into the house?" my mother asked politely.

"Good heavens, no! We lived in Stafford. No, we've just come down to empty the house."

"I believe your aunt has…had…a lot of nice things."

The nephews nodded. They described what was in the house. It sounded like Aladdin's Cave.

Over the next days, we children watched them coming and going, and wished we could join in. Most of the stuff was taken away in a huge furniture van. They also had a smaller van which took away all the rubbish that their aunt had refused to get rid of, mostly great bundles of newspapers. My bother Alan asked the nephews if he could have one of the bundles of newspapers. We read the headline on the top newspaper: "RUSSIAN TANKS ROLL INTO BUDAPEST". It was dated 10 November 1956! Alan took out his penknife and cut the string with which the bundle was tied. We spread the newspapers out, curious to read about things that had happened over fifty years ago.

"What's this?" said Alice, holding something she had found inside the top newspaper.

"Here's another!" said Alan, opening the second newspaper in the bundle.

"And another! And another!" I shouted, as I worked my way through the newspapers.

"What are they? They look like paintings without frames."

This bundle alone contained twenty-five beautiful paintings. We later learned that they were originals, worth at least £500 each. By the time the nephews learned of our discovery, they had already thrown out most of the hundreds of bundles of newspapers.

返璞归真

[西班牙]费尔南多·索伦蒂诺

我很容易接受社会学家或心理分析学家在电视圆桌会议上提出的任何想法。从眼镜、胡须和烟斗喷出的烟雾中浮现出的深沉而无可争辩的男性声音声称,现代人类已经被一点一点地异化了,消费者社会正在消费着人类。

我吓了一跳,心里感到眩晕——这在描述上毫无意义,但很容易想象得到——于是我赶快关掉电视,赶往我住的乌尔基萨别墅附近的苏索里奥·赫马诺斯自行车店。我不知道有多少个苏索里奥兄弟,那时店里只有一个很瘦的高颧骨男人,他人很聪明,办事快捷高效。

当他把自行车卖给我的时候,他说了几句类似老师会对弟子说的话:

"这是你能做的最好的事情。生活变得无可救药得复杂。而自行车却很简单,虽说它只是一种机械装置,但也需要自然的元素:新鲜的空气、阳光以及锻炼。"

我表示赞同。宛若孩子般快乐,我骑着自行车来到了乌尔基萨别墅和普耶雷敦别墅坐落的街道上。几分钟后,我骑到了林奇别墅、桑托斯卢加雷斯和帕洛马尔。"太棒了,"我自言自语道,"这种简单又费力的交通工具让我在短时间内走过这么长的路。"确实是啊,但我到底走了多远呢?

因为我憎恨不精确和猜测,于是我又去见了苏索里奥先生。这一次,他严肃地看着我,充满了不确定,他的态度似乎发生了明显的转变:

"记住,"他说,"回来是你的主意。"

我的回答带有警句式的奉承意味:

"满意的客户总会回到诚实的商人那里。"

我问他是否认为给自行车加里程计是个改进的好主意。

他责备我说:"没有速度表的里程计就像没有刀的叉子,两者相辅相成,给了彼此存在的理由。里程表会告诉你已经走了多远,速度表会告诉你的骑行能力有多强。"

我承认他是对的。几分钟后,这两个装置就装在了我自行车的车把上。

"人们到处闲逛,要么沉浸在自己的世界里,要么就是天生的傻瓜。"苏索里奥先生说,"所以说,你要是遇到心不在焉的人,不要惊讶。要不要安电喇叭来吹个绝妙的三重奏呀?"

"抱歉我不赞同你的意见,我讨厌喇叭声。"

"这个喇叭产自日不落帝国,"他讲道,"也许你知道日本人试图在节省空间。这喇叭还没有火柴盒大,就算你不喜欢城市里喇叭的声音,你仍然可以享受额外的服务:一个带卡式录音和录音机的音箱,一个显示东京、亚的斯亚贝巴和特古西加尔巴官方时间的钟面式风向指示器,一个温度和大气压力指示器及一个具有57个功能的迷你计算器,以备你需要在路上计算路程。"

考虑到这些特点,我很高兴地买了个喇叭。

"天气怎么样?"苏索里奥先生接着问。

这是一个反问句。

"天气好极啦,阳光灿烂的日子。"他自问自答道,"布宜诺斯艾利斯一月的太阳,会灼伤任何一个有幸拥有大脑的人。但是,当你在最荒凉的地方遇上一场猛烈的狂风暴雨,穿着灌有一千加仑水的衣服和鞋子回家时,不要感到惊讶。"

我困惑了一会儿。

他补充道:"在21世纪初,有了这个小装置,只要不是白痴,谁会想让自己淋湿呢?"他手心里托着一台极小的电视。"它能提前72小时预测天气变化,不会有误差。"

他迅速地把它拧到车把上。

"它还显示了澳大利亚和加蓬的等压线和等雨量线,为您提供波斯湾潮汐的信息,并有超声波系统,可以消灭沿路上等待骑行者的豪猪、野狗和鬣蜥。"

"那蚊子和苍蝇呢?"

"非常不幸,这些令人厌恶的双翅昆虫已经对这种装置的光线产生了免疫。但是,当它可以打印单面或双面、彩色和任何纸张上的文件时,能否防蚊子和苍蝇又有什么关系呢?"

由于我花了很多时间复印文件,这项功能深得我心。

"后挡泥板,"苏索里奥先生说,"不应该觉得比车把差。车把上有这么多神奇装置,可后面却空空如也。"

他安装了一个黄油盘大小的金属盒子,车座后面有按钮和控制杆:

"你有点懒惰,可能吃得有些多。当在途中感到有强烈的饥饿感时,有什么能比这个红外线烤炉更好?它能在25秒内做出烤鸡或是土豆烤牛肉,而蒸馏器将空气中的水分转化成勃艮第葡萄酒。"

这个提议很诱人，我根本无力抵抗。

"我出生在这个小镇上，我在乌尔基萨别墅住了53年，"他提高了音量，举起右臂解释道，"我一直觉得我们这个社区就像个大家庭。你看起来不是个卑鄙的人，所以我冒险相信你是个诚实的人。我给你美元计的信用证，36个月分期付清即可。不用麻烦你去我的实验室，把你的地址给我，虽然我已经熟记于心了，明天我的财务经理会带着一些文件去你家让你签字。"

我哆哆嗦嗦地把地址写在报纸边上。怕他忘记自己的承诺，我敦促道：

"他明天一定会来，对吧？"

"他当然会。他会带着期票，迫切需要你的破产签名，还会带着其他标注严谨的预付款项，这些都会让你大吃一惊。我再次祝贺你，这是你能做的最好的事情。生活变得无可救药得复杂，而自行车却很简单而自然。"

我感激涕零地回答："非常感谢。"

我骑着车走了：幸福快乐，充满活力，嘴里还哼着歌。

Going Back to Our Roots

By Fernando Sorrentino

  I tend to instantly accept any idea proposed by a sociologist or psychoanalyst during televised round tables. Emerging among eyeglasses, beards and pipe smoke, the deep and indisputable male voice propounded that modern humans have been objectified and that little by little, the consumer society has been consuming them.

  I got scared and a dizzying mental process—which there is no point in describing, but which is easily imagined—propelled me to immediately turn off the television and hurry to the Suasorio Hermanos bicycle shop in my neighborhood of Villa Urquiza. I do not know how many Suasorio brothers there are as there was only one very thin man with high cheekbones in the shop; he turned out to be clever, efficient and quick.

  As he was selling me the bicycle, he let fall a few sentences of the kind a teacher would say to a disciple:

  "This is the best thing you could have done. Life has become hopelessly complicated. A bicycle is simple, and even though it is a mechanical device, it entails natural things: fresh air, sunshine and exercise."

I agreed. Feeling rather childishly happy, I got on the bicycle and headed out on the streets of Villa Urquiza and Villa Pueyrredón; after a few minutes I ended up in Villa Lynch, in Santos Lugares, in El Palomar. "Amazing," I said to myself. "This simple and ascetic vehicle lets me cover long distances in a fairly short time." Yes, but how far did I really go?

Since I abhor imprecision and conjecture, I went to see Mr. Suasorio again. This time he looked at me with a serious and uncertain air; there seemed to be a perceptible shift in his attitude:

"Remember," he said, "it was your idea to come back."

I answered with sententious flattery:

"A satisfied customer always returns to an honest merchant."

I asked whether he thought it would be a good idea to improve the bicycle with an odometer.

He scolded me: "An odometer without a speedometer is like a fork without a knife; they complement each other and one gives the other a reason to exist. The odometer will tell you how far you've traveled and the speedometer will let you know how strong your riding capabilities are."

I admitted he was right and in a few minutes, the two devices were attached to the handlebars of my bicycle.

"People wander about engrossed in themselves or they are

born fools," said Mr. Suasorio. "So don't be surprised if you run into some absent minded person. How about an electric horn to round out a terrific trio?"

"I'm sorry to disagree with you, but I hate the honking of horns."

"This horn comes from the Empire of the Rising Sun," he lectured, "and perhaps you know that the Japanese try to save space. This is no larger than a matchbox and even if you don't appreciate the melody of a honking urban horn, you can still enjoy the extras: a boom box with cassette player and recorder, a wind clock showing the official time in Tokyo, Addis Ababa and Tegucigalpa, a temperature and atmospheric pressure indicator and a fifty-seven function mini calculator in case you need to do sums along the way."

Given all those features, I was very happy to buy the horn.

"What about the weather?" asked Mr. Suasorio next.

It was a rhetorical question.

"It's wonderful, a radiant day," he answered himself. "January in Buenos Aires fries the brains of anyone lucky enough to have any. But don't be surprised when you get caught in a savage storm in the most desolate spot and return home with a thousand gallons of water in your clothes and shoes."

I puzzled for a moment.

He added, "On the threshold of the 21st century, would

anyone who is not an idiot let himself get wet when there is this little device?" He held a kind of Lilliputian television set in the palm of his hand. "It predicts changes in weather seventy two hours in advance and with zero margin of error."

He rapidly screwed it onto the handlebars.

"It also shows isobars and isohyets for Australia and Gabon, gives you information on tides in the Persian Gulf and has an ultrasonic system that exterminates the porcupines, wild dogs and iguanas that lie in wait for cyclists on the roads."

"What about mosquitoes and flies?"

"Unfortunately, the despicable dipterans have developed immunity to the foolproof rays of this device. But what does that matter, when it also makes copies that are one or two sided, in color and on any kind of paper?"

Since I spend so much time making copies, this feature won me over.

"The rear fender," noted Mr. Suasorio, "shouldn't feel inferior to the handlebars. There are all these wonders on the handlebars and nothing in the back."

He mounted a butter dish sized metal box with buttons and levers behind the seat:

"You're a bit of a slacker and you probably over-eat and enjoy your food. When fierce hunger pangs strike on route, is there anything better than this infrared oven for roasting a chicken or a cut of beef with potatoes and onions in only twenty-five seconds while the distillers turn the moisture in the air into Burgundy wine?"

The offer was tempting and I was not strong enough to resist.

"I was born in this town; I've lived in Villa Urquiza for fifty three years," he proffered, raising his voice and his right arm, "and I have always thought that the neighborhood is like a big family. You don't look sneaky, so I'll risk it and trust that you're honest. I'll give you credit in dollars, to be paid off in thirty-six easy monthly installments. To save you the trouble of going to my laboratory, give me your address, which I already know by heart, and tomorrow my financial manager will go to your house with some documents for you to sign."

I shakily wrote the address in the margin of a newspaper. Fearing he would forget his promise, I urged:

"He will come tomorrow for sure, right?"

"Of course he'll come. He'll be bearing promissory notes crying out for bankrupt signatures and brochures for other scientific advances that will make your jaw drop. I congratulate you once more; this is the best thing you could have done. Life has become hopelessly complicated and a bicycle is simple and natural."

Moved, I answered, "Thank you so much."

I mounted and pedaled away: happy, full of life and with a song on my lips.

代 价

他把手伸进口袋里。

口袋里有一把刀,大约 6 英寸长,尖锐而锋利。握刀的那只手冷冰冰的,不住地颤抖。

哦,上帝,帮帮我吧!他全心全意地祈祷着,请帮我渡过这次难关吧,为此,我愿意付出任何代价。

今天晚上,月亮非常圆。但他抬起头来,看到的却不是月亮,而是托尼那圆圆的、可爱的脸庞。托尼才 4 岁,但他却懂事得让人心疼。两个月以前,托尼的妈妈离家出走了,没有人知道她去了哪里。从那时起,托尼就变得成熟起来,仿佛一夜之间长大成人。他不再像以前那样吵闹、生事了,即便在他做得对的时候也不了。作为他的爸爸,对于他的瞬间成熟,他感到特别奇怪。

他在一家公司做仓库管理员,省吃俭用,靠微薄的收入来维持全家的生活。但是半年前,公司破产了,他也丢了工作。如今,全国经济形势不佳,到处都在裁员。他没有文化,也没有特殊技能,在这样的境况下,怎么才能再找一份工作呢?他的妻子,年轻,脾气不好,不懂得体谅人,她觉得他给的钱不够花,因此,她跟他吵架,又哭又闹,又蹦又跳,最后拿着自己的东西离开了他们父子俩。

妻子离家之后,他就放下自尊,能借的都借了,能求的都求了。

借他钱的人声称他们只是看在孩子的面上才借给他的。然而，正是孩子才让他更难找工作。就在他觉得要垮掉的时候，儿子患上了肺炎，半夜时分被送到了医院。现在儿子已经住院四天了，但他不敢去医院看他，因为他没钱支付医药费和住院费。

这个孩子就是这个家庭的命，不能扔下他不管。

他手里握着刀，满身冒冷汗。

"就这一次。我只做一次！上帝啊，帮帮我吧！我愿为我的行为付出任何代价。"他再次祈求道。

这是一条僻静的小巷。他发现有些人回家都要经过这里。如果在这里抢劫，方便他逃走。因为这条巷子里有很多岔路，只要他灵活地转向，就很容易逃跑。他已经制定好了几条逃跑路线。

昨天晚上，11点之后，共有五个人回家经过这条小巷，但是没有一个是他理想的猎物。他不敢抢劫男人，又觉得不应该抢老人。这样一来，他的目标就只剩下中年妇女了。

今晚，他似乎还是得不到好运气的垂青。他拿着一张报纸站在入口处路灯下面，假装在读报，实际上却在偷偷地盯着小巷里来来往往的人。一、二、三……全都是男人。

11点45分时，啊，好运终于来了。一位45岁左右的中年妇女下了公交车。手上提着一个沉甸甸的包，她腋下有一个旧的黄色钱包。他听到身体里发出"砰砰"的鼓声：噗噗，噗噗，噗噗……他的心猛烈地跳着，感觉要爆炸、撕裂了。

女人走进小巷时，他把报纸扔了，像猫一样蹑手蹑脚地跟着她。

小巷很长，月亮很亮。这个女人突然从地上看到了他的影子，也意识到自己被人跟踪了。她吓得加快了步伐。

他不能失去这样的好机会！他立刻向她扑去，一只手抓着她的肩膀,另一只手捂着她的嘴,对她说:"别动!别喊!我只想要钱。"

女人吓得魂飞魄散、目瞪口呆,不知所措地愣在那里,钱包和背包掉在了地上,动静很大。

他也很慌乱,恐吓道:"别动!我不会伤害你的!"

她用力点了点头。他松开了手。没想到,那女人突然跪在他面前,哭着哀求他说:"可怜可怜我吧,大叔!我包里的钱是借来支付我孩子医疗费的!"

孩子?医疗费?他就像被雷击中一样,脑子里嗡嗡作响。与此同时,托尼那圆圆的、可爱的脸浮现在他面前。他以最快的速度捡起袋子,按照事先计划好的路线逃跑了,留下那个女人,她哭天抢地的恸哭声在寂静的夜晚中回响。

他刚到家,就用被子盖住了自己,浑身颤抖。他尽力来抑制住想哭的冲动。电话响了好几次,但他没有接。

午夜两点,一声刺耳的门铃在他的耳边响起。他从被子里跳出来,冲到门口。他从猫眼向外看,不禁惊恐万状,目瞪口呆,汗如雨下:他家门口站着一名警察。

警察怎么这么快就找到我了!

他迷迷糊糊,头晕目眩,不能再多想了。

同时,门铃又响了起来。

他要崩溃了,然后打开了门。

警察手上没有拿手铐,而是温柔地看着他,然后用平静的语调问:"安德鲁先生在家吗?"

"我就是。"他机械地回答道。

"我来是告诉你,你的孩子昨晚11点45分去世了。"

孩子?11点45分死了?

他突然觉得自己的脚不能再支撑他的身体了。他晕了过去。当他跌倒的时候,听到从遥远的天空传来一个声音:"你说过你愿意付出任何代价。"

The Price

He put his hand in the pocket.

A knife was there, of about six inches long, pointed and sharp. The hand holding it was cold and shivering.

Oh, God, give me a hand! He prayed whole-heartedly, help me get through this difficult situation, and I will pay any price for it!

This night, the moon was quite round. Looking up, he didn't see the moon but Tony's round and lovely face. Tony was only four years old but distressingly understanding. Two months ago, Tony's mother left home, and nobody knew where she went. Since then, the little boy suddenly became mature as if he had grown up overnight. The boy was no longer noisy and deliberately provocative, even if he was in the right. As his father, he felt terribly strange about the boy's sudden maturity.

He was a storehouse warder. With his frugality, he managed the whole family's life on his meager income. Half a year ago, his company went bankrupt, and as a result, he lost his job. Now the economy wasn't good nation-wide and the stuff reduction occurred everywhere. Being illiterate and having no special sills, how could he find a new job in such a situation? His wife, young, hot-tempered and not understanding, found that she couldn't get money from him, so she quarreled, cried, shouted, jumped, and packed all she had and left them at last.

After she left, he sold out all his dignity he borrowed what he could borrow, asked for and begged for what he could beg for. All those who lent him money claimed that they did it for the sake of the kid. However, it was the kid who made his job-hunting more difficult. When he was about to collapse, his son suffered from pneumonia and was sent to hospital at midnight. Now his son had been staying in the hospital for four days but he dared not go to see him, because he had no money to pay for the medicine and hospitalization expenses.

The child was the very life of the family and shouldn't be left uncared for.

His hand holding the knife was sopped with sweat.

"Only once. I'll do it just once! God, help me! I would pay any price for my behavior!" He prayed again.

This was a quiet alley. He had detected that some people always went back home through this alley. If he robbed someone here it would be easy for him to flee away, for there were several turnoffs which were convenient for him to escape so long as he made some adroit turns. He even had planned his routes for escape.

Last night, after eleven o'clock, there were altogether five people returning home via this alley, but none was his ideal prey. He dared not rob the men, should not rob the old. He could only target at those middle-aged women.

Tonight, it seemed that good lucks still didn't show appreciation for him. Holding a piece of newspaper, he stood under the streetlamp at the entrance to the alley and pretended to read it, with his eyes staring at everyone to and fro. One, two, three…all of them were men.

At eleven forty-five, oh, it came! A middle-aged woman of about forty years old got down the bus. She held a heavy bag with one hand and under her armpit was an old yellow purse. He heard a primitive drum thumping within his body: "flop", "flop", "flop"…His heart was beating so violently that he felt his whole chest was going to explode and split up.

When the woman stepped into the alley, he threw off the newspaper and followed her like a cat.

The alley was long and the moon was very bright. The woman suddenly found the shadow on the ground and realized she was followed. In great terror, she sped up.

He couldn't lose such a good chance! He threw himself upon her at once, one hand grasping her shoulder and the other covering her mouth. Lowering his voice, he said to her, "Don't move! Don't cry! I only want money!"

Greatly terrified, she froze there, dumbfounded. Her purse and bag fell onto the ground, producing a loud sound.

He was also flurried and scared, "Don't move! I won't hurt you!"

She nodded with great strength. He loosened his hand. Unexpectedly, the woman abruptly knelt down in front of him and begged him sobbingly, "Please be merciful, uncle! The money in my bag was borrowed for paying for my child's medical expenses!"

Child? Medical expenses? As if stricken by thunders, he felt his buzzing, meanwhile, Tony's round and lovely face turned up in front of him. Picking up the bag as quickly as possible, he ran away according to the route planned in advance, leaving the woman behind, whose wailing cries spread and echoed in the quiet night.

Hardly had he got home when he covered himself with a quilt, trembling a lot. He took great efforts to suppress his impulse to cry. The telephone rang several times but he didn't answer it.

At two o'clock in the midnight, a harsh doorbell ringing pierced into his ears. He jumped out of the quilt and rushed to the door. Looking out from the door hole, he got scared and shocked. He couldn't help opening his mouth and sweat streamed down his face. A policeman was at his door.

How can he be so quick!

Confused and dizzy, he could no longer contemplate.

At this time, the doorbell rang again.

Collapsed, he opened the door.

With no cuffs in his hand, the policeman looked at him gently and said in a calm tone.

"Is Mr. Andrew at home?"

"I am." He answered automatically.

"I come here to inform you that your child died at eleven forty-five last night."

Child? Died at eleven forty-five?

He suddenly felt his feet could no longer support his body. He fainted away. As he was falling down, he heard a voice coming from afar in the sky, "You said you would rather pay any price."

轮到你了，轮到你了

[英国] 史蒂文 D. 杰克逊

我现在写着这个，是因为我没有别的选择了。我想说这是对其他人的一个警告，但我有更自私的理由。即使我警告你了，但我还是怀疑你是否会注意到，因为我就没有注意到别人给我的警告。我不能再浪费时间了，因为时间在浪费我，从某种程度上来说，这违背了我曾经相信和熟悉的医学科学。在我写的时候，我的关节很疼，我知道不久我就没法继续写了。但是我必须要告诉其他人，所以我得继续写。

我是紫檀小屋的一名医生，看起来很老成，但是我今年才27岁。你读到这些文字的时候你几乎想象不到昨天的我是什么样子的。

在我来之前，紫檀小屋没有住院医师。远离我接受培训并取得认证资格的医院，这是我人生的第一个大突破。面试的时候，我说我不计报酬，所以他们都抢着要我。

紫檀小屋是一家老年患者福利院，一些患者的护理需求比普通养老院更高。所以董事会决定，花钱雇佣像我这样的人，比把钱花在请顾问、不断处理紧急情况上更具有经济意义。

总而言之，这份工作很棒。轻松但也要负责任。富有挑战性，但也容易掌控。最后，给的工资也足够我最终买套公寓。

这个护理中心实际上是一栋三层的独立公寓，每层分三个区，分别是：A区、B区和C区。一些住处不像"公寓"，而是有很多房间，没有锁，也没有真正的配套设施。护士和社会服务人员都想离我远一点，因为我对他们来说还是一个局外人，这个地方毕竟是由他们管理的，每天都跟这里的"常驻人员"见面，而我只有在他们生病的时候才过去。

然而，我从同事那里得到了一个奇怪的警告，说二楼B区尽头17号房间里有一个男人。这个警告比较荒谬之处在于每个区只有16个房间。护士们对此的反应也趋向于奇怪，说如果有17号房间，我最好不要进去。我觉得没什么，一笑而过，很快就把这件事忘得一干二净了。

直到有一天，我碰巧在二楼的B区发现了一个我以前没见过的房间，可是为时已晚，我已经在紫檀小屋工作三天了。我一直在走廊的一个房间里照顾着一个需要好好观察的病人。我正在考虑早上把他送去临终安养院，我看了看他的病历，觉得那里更适合他。所以当我离开他的房间，转身上楼梯的时候，我的心情并不好。

我不知道是我心情不好的缘故，还是时间太晚了，但有某种东西让我停下了脚步。我感到脖子后面一阵刺痛，有一种毛骨悚然的、不太对劲的感觉。我转过身。我后来多么希望我没有转身。我多希望我当时能继续走，沿着灯火通明的走廊，下楼回到我的办公室啊！相反，我回头看了看大厅。在那里，头顶上闪烁的灯光在远处的墙上投下了黑色的影子，窗框显得更亮了，伸入远处的黑暗之中。

模模糊糊、闪闪烁烁的灯光下，我瞥见了一扇本不该在那里出现的门。我知道它不应该出现在那里，我当时的确想起了那个警告，但老实说，我太好奇了，并坚定地相信科学和理性，无法视而不见。我走近那扇门，好奇心胜过了我的疑心。直到我的手指放到雕刻精美的数字17的门把手上，我甚至没有感觉到一丝丝恐惧。门把手死一样的冰冷，我战战兢兢地把手缩了回来。

我咒骂自己是个愚蠢的孩子,开始认为这完全是护士们的恶作剧。我抬头看了看天花板的一角,希望在某个地方看到一台摄像机。一想到自己可能变成了一个傻瓜,我就下定了决心,把手包在袖子里打开了门。接下来的那一瞬间,我不禁呆住了。制造一扇恶作剧的门是一回事,把它打开就是另一回事了。里面有一个我知道一小时前并不存在的房间。

与其他房间一样,里面也是一个住人的房间。右墙旁边有一个小厨房,左边挨着门处有一间小浴室、一张咖啡桌和一台电视。沿着对面的墙有一张床一直到大窗户下,电视机前摆了一张皮质沙发。沙发上坐着一个老人,从后面我正好可以看到他的头顶,一缕灰白的头发散在沙发上。

我本应该跑的。我本应该停下的。我应该遵从这些本能,本能让我们保持理智、保命。但我生来就是为了寻求领悟和理性的,我决定去看看到底发生了什么。

我走到老人跟前,空气中弥漫着老式药的味道,还有人身体长期没有洗过澡的味道。给我的印象是有很长一段时间都没有人打扰过他。只有气若游丝的喘息声说明他还在呼吸。当我走近,映入眼帘的是他满脸的皱纹和睁开了的乳白色的蓝眼睛。老人的手指放在沙发的扶手上,微微抽搐着。他的嘴微微动了动,他的呼吸成了一个响板,他好像要说话。他给我的印象是很激动,是因为我的出现还是因为别的什么,我说不好,不过,他也没有能力挪动。

我坐在他沙发旁边的脚凳上,当我看见他苍白的皮肤、薄薄的开裂的嘴唇、颤抖的手指时,我就在大脑里对他进行诊断。他似乎有脱水的症状,身体虚弱,由于肌肉萎缩,所以瘦骨嶙峋,但是他还穿着衣服，看上去并没有弄脏自己。一定是有人在照顾他，也许是其中的一名护士？是不是他们把他关在这里，这个秘密被我意外地发现了？

这个男人的目光投向咖啡桌上面的一本书上，目不转睛地盯着，然后偷偷地、迅速地向我瞥了一眼。凭直觉，我觉得他想要那本书。这是一本薄薄的、牛皮做的大部头图书，上面用细长的字母标注的日期是1916年。我拿起书，然后把书放在他的膝盖上。他直勾勾地盯着我，又盯着那本书，然后又盯着我。

于是我又拿起书，这很明显是一本日记，我看了看最后一篇文章。

"1916年4月25日。"我大声地读道。有点惊讶的是，这和今天的日期相同，只不过是一百年前。老人睁大眼睛直勾勾地盯着我。我继续往下读。

"我的关节痛得要命……我没希望了。当我试图逃跑的时候，这座可怕的建筑房门很快地锁上了，走廊里还有我不敢说出名字的幽灵看守。我唯一的退路就是这儿，这个本不可能存在的房间。每走一步，我都觉得我的身体更虚弱了，我别无选择，只能坐下来，但现在我也不能从凳子上站起来了。我的手指几乎抓不住这根笔。我觉得我的老年在拥抱着我，就像一个不需要的情人，每一秒都在夺去我的时间……"

书页上的字变得难以辨认，笔尖在纸张上面的划痕说明了书写者的痛苦。这些划痕在纸的另一边集中起来了，用大大的字母写的大写字在这页上行进着，仿佛是对马上到来的动弹不得的反抗。

"……那个沉默的人走了……我是他的替代者……时间不多了……愿上帝原谅我……"

我从凳子上站起来，心脏在胸口狂跳。我跌跌撞撞地离开那个沉默的人，差点儿跌倒在凳子上，我心乱如麻，充满了悬疑和恐惧。他还在睁大眼睛看着我，但现在我在他的眼睛里看到了其他的东西。一种可怕的希望，一种期待，我担心我已经知道了原因。我对科学和医学的信仰、理性都从我身上飞走了，被纯恐惧的翅膀带走了。

我没再多想就逃出了房间。门关上的时候，我高兴得说不出话来，在闪闪烁烁的灯光下我又回到了走廊。我跑向楼梯，疯狂地跑回让我感到宽慰的办公室、我的电脑、我的生活，超越了这种不可能。我在拐角处稍做停留。

在我面前，走廊的尽头，站着一个老妇人。她穿着一件脏兮兮的白色病号服，弯腰驼背得厉害，脑袋埋在一头乱蓬蓬的、灰白的头发下，头发几乎垂到地上。她用一只皱巴巴的手抓住她静脉滴注器的金属杆，就像古代战场上的旗手一样。我看见她的时候，我就知道在紫檀小屋这儿没有这样的病人。我头顶的灯熄灭了，走廊都陷入了黑暗。老妇人头顶的灯忽明忽暗。她笨拙地拖着脚步走了一段，好像被笼罩在头顶的黑暗弄得焦虑不安，抑或觉得自由自在。灯灭了。她随即出现在我的眼前，在我头顶上方的灯光照明的边缘，就好像她只在黑暗的地方存在。她的身上散发着湿衣服的恶臭和发霉的奶酪的臭味，我猛地往后退，想离不可能存在的她远一点。我头顶的灯闪了一下。我转过身赶紧跑，有生命危险，所以我加快了速度。我试着开了开左边的门，但是锁上了。我又试了试右边，也锁上了。我身后的那个老妇人发出了一种可怕的咯咯笑声，她头顶上的灯灭了，随即出现在离我几米远的地方。

我不停地跑，但突然感觉到四肢疼痛，呼吸比之前困难得多，跑的时候还绊倒了。

不久，我又跑回了这个不可能存在的房间，正如我所害怕的那样，房间里那个老人已经消失了。我大喊大叫，尖叫咒骂着，但是，正如我所知道的那样，萎缩感缓缓向我袭来。关节的疼痛就像火在我的骨头里燃烧，运动的痛苦和运动本身一样让人疲惫。我撑不住了，于是拖着筋疲力尽的身体,倒在了我现在坐的椅子上。我用最后的力气打了这些字,很快,我就要被压垮了,但在此之前,我必须采取行动,然后我才能像我的"前任"那样等待着陷入昏迷。为了加快发布速度,我必须把我的故事上传到网上的读者能看到的任何地方。在我拿手机打字的时候,感觉手指被灼伤,但是我的绝望却给了我力量让我忽视掉疼痛,忽视掉将这个诅咒继续传下去的负疚感。

所以,我感谢正在看着这些的你。

接下来,你即将感到的痛苦将是你的故事的开始,却是我的故事的结尾。

It's Your Turn, It's Your Turn

By Steven D. Jackson

I am writing this because I have no choice. I'd like to say it is a warning to others, but I have far more selfish reasons. Even if I did warn you, I doubt you would heed it, as I did not heed the warning left for me. I must not waste time, as time is wasting me, in a way that defies the medical science I once believed I knew. My joints ache as I write, and soon I know I will be unable to continue. Yet this must be told and so I write on.

I am a doctor here at Rosewood Lodge, and I am twenty-seven years old though I look older. And by the time you read this it will be scarcely possible for you to imagine me as I was yesterday.

Before me, Rosewood had no resident doctor. This was my first big break, away from the hospital where I'd trained and qualified. At the interview I pretty much said I'd work for anything, so they snapped me up.

Rosewood is a residential care home for elderly patients, some of whose care needs had started to become more advanced than those which a nursing home can ordinarily provide. The board had decided that, rather than paying out for consultants and continually dealing with emergencies, it made better economic sense to have someone like me on the payroll.

It was, in short, an excellent job. Relaxed, but responsible. Challenging, but manageable. And the money was good enough for me to get my own flat, finally.

The home is essentially three storeys of self-contained flats, divided into three wings, A, B and C on each floor. Some residences are less "flats" and more rooms, without locks and without any real facilities of their own. The nurses and social workers tended to stay away from me, as I was still an outsider to them, and they had the run of the place, working with the residents each day whereas I would only see them if they were ill.

One thing that I did pick up from my colleagues however was the strange warning about the man in the room 17 on the end of wing B on the second floor. The ridiculous thing about that particular warning was that the numbers on each wing only go up to 16. The nurses tended to act strangely about it, saying that if ever there was a room 17 I'd be better off not going in. I saw no harm in laughing along with it at the time, and I quickly forgot all about it.

Until the day I happened to be in B wing on the second floor and noticed a room I hadn't seen before. I had been at Rosewood for three days, and it was late. I'd been tending to a particularly unwell man in a room along the corridor, who'd needed a lot of attention. I was considering referring him to a hospice in the morning, if after I studied his charts I decided they would be better placed to care for him. So I wasn't really in a good frame of mind as I left his room and turned to make my way to the stairs.

I don't know if it was my mood, or the lateness of the hour, but something made me stop. I felt a tingle at the back of my neck, a creeping sense of something not right. I turned. How I wish I had not. I wish I had kept on, along the brightly lit corridor, down the stairs and back to my office. Instead I looked back along the hall to where a flickering overhead light cast dark shadows over the far wall, highlighting the steel edges of the window looking out into the blackness beyond.

Glimpsed for moments at a time in that uncertain light was a door that should not have been there. I knew it should not have been there, and I did recall the warning, but truthfully I was too intrigued and too steadfast in my belief in science and rationality to ignore it. I approached it, curiosity overcoming my incredulity. I did not feel even the faintest stirrings of fear until my fingers touched the handle beneath the elegantly carved number 17. It was deathly cold, and I pulled my hand back with trepidation.

Cursing myself for a foolish child, and beginning to believe it was all some kind of prank by the nursing staff, I glanced up at the ceiling half expecting to see a camera propped up somewhere. The thought that perhaps I was being made a fool steeled my resolve, and wrapping my hand in my sleeve I opened the door. For a moment I was stunned. It was one thing to make a prank door, quite another to make it open. And beyond lay a room that I knew had not existed an hour before.

Inside was a residential room like any other. A small kitchenette along one wall to the right, next to a door to a small bathroom, a coffee table and a TV along the left. A bed stretched along the far wall beneath large windows, and a sofa sat facing the TV. Poking out above the sofa I could just about see the top of an old man's head, wisps of grey hair draped across the leather.

I should have run. I should have quit. I should have obeyed those instincts which keep us all sane and alive. But I'd made a lifetime out of understanding and reason, and I was determined to find out what was happening.

I approached the old man, the scent of old medicine and unwashed bodies thick in the air. I had the impression that he had not been disturbed for a very long time. Only a faint, wheezing rasp indicated that he was breathing. Milky blue eyes widened in a withered and lined face as I came into view, and the old man's fingers, resting against the leather chair's arms, twitched slightly. His mouth moved a little and his breathing became a rattle, as though he was trying to speak. I had the impression that he was agitated, by my presence or by something else I could not tell, but that he was also powerless to move.

I sat down on the footstool by his chair, running through diagnoses in my head as I took in the pallor of his skin, the thin cracked lips, the struggling fingers. He seemed to be dehydrated, weak and wasted through muscle atrophy, and yet he was clothed and appeared not to have soiled himself. Someone must have been looking after him then, perhaps one of the nurses? Had they been keeping him here, a secret only revealed by some accident?

The man's eyes drifted to a book lying on the coffee table and seized upon it, glancing back to me only in short furtive motions. Intuiting that he wanted it I picked it up, a thin leathery tome with the date 1916 written upon it in spidery letters, and placed it on his knees. He stared at me, back at the book, then at me.

So I picked it up again, and turned to the last entry of what was clearly a diary.

"April 25th, 1916," I read aloud, somewhat astonished that it was the same date as today, only one hundred years before. The old man stared at me through wide eyes. I continued to read.

"My joints seize with pain...there is no hope for me. The doors of this infernal building were locked fast against me when I tried to flee, the corridors guarded by spectres I dare not name. My only retreat is here. This impossible room that should not be. With every step I felt my body crippled further, and I had no choice but to sit, yet now I cannot rise from my chair. My fingers can barely hold this pen. I feel age embracing me like an unwanted lover, taking years from me with each passing second…"

The words on the page became illegible, the scratching of the pen a testament to the writer's pain. Further down the page they rallied, large letters in capital letters marching across the page as though in defiance of his pending immobility.

"…the silent man is gone…I am his replacement…time is short…god forgive me…"

I rose from the stool, my heart thumping wildly within my chest. I stumbled and almost fell over the stool as I moved away from the silent man, my thoughts a jumble of half-finished fears. The wide eyes watched me still, but now I saw something else within them. Some kind of grim hope, an expectation, and I feared I knew for what. All my belief in science and medicine, rationality and reason flew from me, carried away on wings of pure terror.

Without another thought I fled the room, glad beyond words when the door yielded, leading me back into the corridor beneath the flickering light. I ran for the stairs, frantically making for the comforts of my office, my computer, my life beyond this impossibility. I stopped short as I rounded the corner.

Before me, at the end of the corridor, stood an old woman. She was in a dirty white hospital robe, and was hunched over to such a degree that her head was hidden beneath a long mop of lank grey hair reaching almost to the ground. In one wrinkled hand she clutched the metal pole of her IV stand like a banner-bearer on an ancient battlefield. As I saw her I knew we had no such patient in Rosewood. Behind her, the remainder of the corridor was plunged into darkness as the overhead light went out. The light above the woman flickered on and off, and she shuffled a little with an awkward motion as though agitated—or freed—by the shadows playing over her. The light went out. Instantly, she was in front of me, at the edge of illumination cast by the light above my head, as though existing only in that dark place beyond. A fetid stench of wet clothes and mouldy cheese radiated from the woman and I recoiled violently, as much from the smell as her sudden impossible appearance. The light above me flickered. I turned and ran, mortal peril lending me speed. I tried the door to the left, but it was locked. I tried the right; locked. The woman behind me uttered a hideous gurgling sound as the light above her died, instantly bringing her a few more metres towards me.

 I kept running, but was suddenly aware of an ache in my limbs. It was harder to breathe than it should have been, and I stumbled as I ran.

 Before long I was driven back to this impossible room, where I discovered that, as I feared, the old man had vanished. I shouted, I screamed, I railed against it, but slowly the atrophy stole over me, as I knew it would. The pain of arthritis grew like fire in my bones, the agony of movement as tiring as the movement itself. I couldn't resist, and I lowered my exhausted body into this chair where I now sit. I have typed these words with the last strength I have, and soon I must succumb, but I must do something before I fall back into the stupor that awaits me as it did my predecessor. To speed my release, I must upload my story to anywhere a reader may find them across the internet. My fingers burn with unnatural pain as I work my phone, but my desperation gives me the strength to ignore it, along with any guilt I might feel at passing on this curse.

And so to you who read this I thank you.

The next ache you feel will be the start of your sentence, and the end of mine.

机器人巴克斯特

[英国] 卡尔·佩兰

我的表妹贝蒂娜转向巴克斯特说:"你为什么不给我们来几瓶啤酒呢?再来点儿奶酪和饼干也不错。"当巴克斯特走向厨房时,她补充道:"别忘了给我拿杯啤酒。"巴克斯特一走出视线之外,她就转向我道:"你不该在午饭后洗碗。"

"这是应该的,"我说,"毕竟,巴克斯特做了午餐。"

她叹了口气。"看在上帝的分儿上,吉米,"她说,"巴克斯特是个机器人,他就该做这些。"

"所有的工作都得由他来做,这似乎不大公平。"

"吉米,吉米,吉米,你让那个机器人占了你的便宜,我注意到你毫无怨言地吃了所有的甘蓝。我知道你一直讨厌甘蓝。"

"巴克斯特说吃甘蓝对我有好处。"

贝蒂娜把她的手放在我的脸颊上。"吉米,你是个老好人,但你必须鼓起勇气,不要让那个机器人对你该做什么指手画脚。"

"他就像一个家人一样。他和我在一起快二十年了。"

贝蒂娜哼了一声,向窗外望去,看着落在草坪上的小雨。"我注意到橱柜里大约有六盒馅饼。你什么时候开始吃这些的?"

"我不吃啊。可是既然巴克斯特买了,你不能对他说'不'。我不想伤害巴克斯特的感情。"

"他是个机器人,吉米。"

这时巴克斯特拿着啤酒和奶酪回到了客厅。贝蒂娜拿起一瓶啤酒,在手里转了转。"我的杯子,巴克斯特。"她说。当他回到厨房时,贝蒂娜说:"还有他给你买的那些淡色衬衫。"

"我承认那不是我常穿的那种衬衫。"

"该死的,我猜就不是。你看起来像个娘炮。我敢打赌,你一定还把它们藏在某个地方了。"

"是的,我可以把它们扔出去,但我不想……"

"我知道。你不想伤害巴克斯特的感情。"

担心伤害机器人的感情可能听起来很傻,但我拥有巴克斯特很长一段时间了,而且随着时间的推移,我做了很多维护工作。我有一次把他的固态硬盘换掉了,甚至把中央处理器也换了。每隔几年就会有一个新的操作系统问世,我总是更新至最新版本。大约5年前,这个新系统在人工智能方面有了很大的发展。从那以后巴克斯特就比我聪明了。因此,我不介意听他的建议,也偶尔让他替我做决定。

最新的操作系统有了一个新功能,使机器人更加同情人类。这个功能仍然是试验性的,需要做一些工作,但我想,没有人是完美的。事实上,我并不认为巴克斯特是一台机器,甚至不是一个仆人,而是一个朋友或同伴,这就是我对待他的方式。

不过,我记得有一次,他做得太过了。我对我的工作不太满意,抱怨老板好几个星期了。巴克斯特就自作主张给我的老板发了电子邮件,说公司应该对我更好。我第二天去上班的时候,我的老板用电子邮件和我对质:"好啊,你不必再担心在这里受到虐待了。你被解雇了。"

我对巴克斯特大发雷霆,但他向我保证,凭我的能力,很快就能找到一份更好的工作。事实上,他帮我找到了一份比以前好得多的新工作。结果一切都好。贝蒂娜离开后,我去厨房看晚饭吃什么。巴克斯特坐在厨房的桌子上玩填字游戏。他看着我说:"你最好换件衣服。你还要带玛丽贝斯·惠特尼去高级餐厅吃饭呢。"

玛丽贝斯是一个和我年龄相仿的邻居。她单身,人很好,但我没什么兴趣和她约会。

"你什么意思?"我问道,"我怎么要带她出去吃晚饭?"

"是我为你安排的。你已经37岁了,该结婚了。已婚男人比单身男人活得更长。另外,我还注意到她对你有意思。"

"你可以打电话给她,告诉她你想说的这一切,但我不会和她约会的。"

我不知道我能不能给巴克斯特买到一个旧的操作系统,一个在机器人变得如此聪明之前就已经开发出来的操作系统。

Baxter

By Carl Perrin

My cousin Bettina turned to Baxter and said, "Why don't you get us a couple of beers. And some cheese and crackers would be nice too." As Baxter moved toward the kitchen, she added, "And don't forget to get me a glass for my beer." Once Baxter was out of sight, she turned to me. "You shouldn't have done the dishes after lunch."

"It just seemed right," I said. "After all, Baxter made the lunch."

She sighed. "For God's sake, Jimmy," she said. "Baxter is a robot. He's supposed to be doing things like that."

"It doesn't seem fair for him to have to do all the work."

"Jimmy, Jimmy, Jimmy, you're letting that robot take advantage of you. I noticed you ate all your Brussels sprouts without complaining. I know you always hated Brussels sprouts."

"Baxter says they're good for me."

Bettina put her hand on my cheek. "Jimmy, you're a sweet

guy, but you've got to grow some balls and stop letting that robot tell you what to do."

"He's almost like family. He's been with me for almost twenty years."

Bettina snorted and looked out the window at the light rain falling on the lawn. "I noticed about six boxes of Pop-Tarts in the cabinet. When did you start eating them?"

"I don't eat them. But Baxter bought them, and you can't say 'no' to him. I don't want to hurt Baxter's feelings."

"He's a robot, Jimmy."

At that point Baxter came back into the living room with the beer and cheese. Bettina picked up one of the beers and twirled it in her hand. "My glass, Baxter," she said. When he went back to the kitchen, Bettina said, "And the time he bought you all those pastel shirts."

"I admit they weren't the kind of shirts I usually wear."

"I guess to hell they weren't. You looked liked a nance. I bet you still have them someplace."

"Yes, I'd throw them out, but I don't want…"

"I know. You don't want to hurt Baxter's feelings."

It probably sounds silly to worry about a robot's feelings, but I had had Baxter for a long time and had done a lot of maintenance over time. I had had his SSD replaced at one time and even his CPU. Every few years a new operating system came out, and I had always updated to the newest system. About five years ago the new system had a big increase in artificial intelligence. After that Baxter was smarter than I was. I didn't mind listening to his advice and letting him make decisions for me once in a while.

The latest operating system had come with a factor that made the robots more empathetic to human beings. That factor was still experimental and needed some work, but I figured, no one is perfect. In truth, I didn't think of Baxter as a machine or even as a servant, but as a friend or companion, and that's the way I treated him.

I remember one time, however, when he went too far. I had been unhappy with my job and complaining about my boss for several weeks. Baxter took it on himself to email my boss to say that the company should be treating me better. When I went to work the next day, my boss confronted me with the email. "Well, you won't have to worry about being mistreated here anymore. You're fired."

I was furious with Baxter, but he reassured me that with my ability, I would be able to get a much better job in no time. In fact he helped me find a new job which is much better than the old one. So it turned out all right in the end. After Bettina left, I went to the kitchen to see what was for dinner. Baxter was sitting at the kitchen table working a crossword puzzle. He looked me and said, "You better change your clothes. You're taking Marybeth

Whitney out to dinner at the Tip Top."

Marybeth was a neighbor about my age. She was single and a nice enough person, but I had no interest in dating her.

"What do you mean?" I demanded. "How come I'm taking her out to dinner?"

"I arranged it for you. You're 37 years old. It's about time you got married. Married men live longer than single men. Besides, I've noticed that she has eyes for you."

"You can call her and tell her anything you want, but I am not going to go on a date with her."

I wondered if I would be able to get one of the old operating systems for Baxter, one of the ones made before the robots got so smart.

星 光

[美国]艾萨克·阿西莫夫

艾萨克·阿西莫夫原是一名科学家,随后又成为一名科幻小说作家。他享誉世界,作品颇丰,以写机器人的故事而家喻户晓。《星光》似乎就是以电脑为主角展开的。然而,正如阿西莫夫从未说明的一样——只有人类才会创造悲剧和灾难,而非机器。特伦特是一名逃犯,他了解这一真相时已经为时过晚!

阿瑟·特伦特听得很真切,激烈、愤怒的词语像枪林弹雨一样,从听筒里射出。

"特伦特!你不能离开,两小时之内我们要进入你的轨道,如果你敢反抗,我们就把你扔进太空。"

特伦特笑而不语,他没有武器,更没有必要反抗。用不了两小时,飞船就会一跃穿过外太空,他们就永远都找不到他了。他必须携带近1公斤的克里林,这足够用以制造数千台机器人的电子神经,其价值大约1000万宇宙货币单位。因此,毫无疑问,只要他一飞降到银河系中任何一颗有太空移民的行星上,摇身一变就是富翁。

老布伦迈耶已经全盘计划好了,他已经为此花费了30多年的时间,可以说这是他的心血之作。

"年轻人,这才刚开始。"他说,"我需要你,因为你能驾驶飞船脱离地面进入太空,而我做不到。"

"布伦迈耶先生,这不是个好主意,"特伦特说,"用不了半天时间我们便会被抓起来。"

"不,"布伦迈耶眼睛一转道,"如果我们一跃而起,而不是在穿越途中的数光年前就停下来。"

"实行计划只需要半天时间,但即使我们抓紧时间,警察也会向所有卫星系统报警。"

"不,特伦特,你错了。"老布伦迈耶激动起来,颤抖的手抓着他的手说,"不会向所有的卫星系统报警,只会向邻近的12个银河系报警。银河系这么大,太空移民早在50000年前相互间就失去了联系。"

他兴致勃勃地说着,描画着这番图景。在史前时期,如今的银河系像原始人的旧星球(人类称之为地球)。人类曾散布整个大陆,但每个群体只熟悉附近的区域。

"如果我们盲目地一跃而起,"布伦迈耶说,"我们将无处不在,哪怕是在50000光年以外,找到我们犹如在流星群中找到一颗鹅卵石一样难。"

特伦特摇了摇头道:"那样的话,我们自己也找不到自己了。我们不能用这么毫无头绪的方式寻找可居住的星球。"

布伦迈耶的眼睛滴溜溜乱转,迅速看了看四周,发现四下无人,可还是压低声音耳语道:"我花了30年时间收集银河系里每一个可居住星球的数据。我搜集了所有昔日的档案。我走过了几千光年的路,比太空宇航员走的都多。每一个可居住星球的位置都存在这世界上最好的电脑内存卡上。"

特伦特礼貌性地挑了下眉毛。

布伦迈耶说："我设计电脑，最好的电脑。我也标记出银河系每颗发光星球的具体位置，它们在光谱上处于F、B、A还是O，统统都记录在内存卡里，一旦我们一跃而起，电脑会用分光镜扫描天空，并结合地图结果进行比较。只要找到合适的路线，迟早会定位到空间飞船的位置并自动导引第二次一跃，跳到最近的一颗星球上。"

"听起来太复杂啦。"

"不容错过。我这些年为此投入了全部，不容错过。我能当百万富翁的时间就剩十年了。但你还年轻，时间更长。"

"如果你盲目地一跃而起，你的命一定会交待在一颗星星里。"

"万无一失，特伦特。我们也可以降落在离发光星球远一些的地方，任何计算机都无计可施，阻止不了这一计划。我们一跃而起一两光年以后，警察可能还被我们甩在后面。就连这种机会都很小，如果你非要担心，还是担心自己会不会在一跃而起时心脏病发作，这个概率反而更高。"

"你才会心脏病发作呢，布伦迈耶先生，你上岁数啦。"

老头耸了耸肩道："我不担心，电脑会自动安排好一切。"

特伦特点了点头，想起一个午夜，飞船准备就绪，布伦迈耶拎着装有克里林的手提箱到达（他没问题，是个靠得住的人）。特伦特一只手提着箱子，另一只手在身体一侧摆动，动作迅速，胸有成竹。

刀子依然是最好的工具，犹如去极化剂分子，一刀致命，杀人于无声。但特伦特把带指纹的刀子留在了身体里。为什么这么做？因为这样他们就抓不到他了。

在太空深处，还有警察的追捕，他无暇顾及紧绷的神经只想着完成跳跃。心理学家恐怕都无法解释，只有每个专业的太空宇航员才能懂得这是什么感受。

那是一种瞬间的、由内而外的感觉,正如他与他的飞船一瞬间地超越时空,变得无物质无能量,随后又立即和银河系中别的部分重新合成。

特伦特笑了,自己还活着。星星之间相隔有度。天空有了星星的点缀显得格外灵动,与他在一跃而起远离之前的图案大不相同。一些恒星只能是 F 型谱或者更好。电脑会有与记忆相配的美好、丰富的图案。这用不了多长时间。

他舒舒服服地向后仰着,随着飞船缓缓地旋转,欣赏着移动的、熠熠生辉的星光图案。有一颗明星进入视线,分外耀眼,不像是在几光年以外,作为领航员的直觉告诉他那是一颗火热的星星。电脑可以把它作为基础和中心,匹配整个图案模型。他又一次想:用不了太长时间了。

可是却用了很长时间。一分钟接着一分钟过去了。他不停歇地敲击着电脑,灯一直闪烁。

特伦特皱了皱眉。为什么找不到图案模型呢?明明就在这里。布伦迈耶给他看过他多年的成果。在他的记录中没落下一颗星星,没标记错任何一颗的位置。

的确,恒星出现、消失、移动,这些都赖以在太空里存在,但这些变化极其缓慢。一百万年间,布伦迈耶的模型恐怕无法……

突然,一阵惶恐向特伦特袭来。不!不可能。这种可能性要比跳到恒星内部小多了。

他在等下一颗明亮的星星出现,用颤抖的双手举着望远镜聚焦。他放到最大倍数,光斑周围是泄露秘密的烟雾湍流气体报警器在飞行途中。

是诺达!

昏暗模糊的天空中,一颗恒星逐渐亮了起来——大概是在一个月以前。它诞生于一个特殊的光谱中,位置很低,电脑无法检测到,但也值得重视。

诺达在太空中存在,电脑的记忆储存里却没有,因为布伦迈耶没有记录。在布伦迈耶收集数据时它还不存在——至少还不是一颗发光星球。

"想都别想!"特伦特尖叫道,"无视它!"

但他咆哮的对象是一台自动的机器,它会匹配诺达中心图案和银河系的图案模型,它会无处不在地持续运行,只要它有能量供应就会一直匹配、匹配、匹配下去。

氧气很快就要吸完了。特伦特快要死了。

特伦特无助地瘫倒在椅子上,看着星星模型的无情嘲笑,他只能开始对死亡漫长而痛苦地等待。

——如果他带上刀子就好了。

Star Light

By Isaac Asimov

Isaac Asimov is a scientist who became a writer of science fiction. His reputation is world-wide and his output enormous. He is particularly well-known for stories about robots. *Star Light* seems to have a computer as a major "character". However, as Asimov never tires of telling us, it is human beings and not machines that cause tragedy and disaster. This truth, Trent, the escaping criminal, learns too late!

Arthur Trent heard them quite clearly. The tense, angry words shot out of his receiver.

"Trent! You can't get away. We will intersect your orbit in two hours and if you try to resist we will blow you out of space."

Trent smiled and said nothing. He had no weapons and no need to fight. In far less than two hours the ship would make its jump through hyperspace and they would never find him. He would have with him nearly a kilogram of Krillium, enough for the construction of the brain-paths of thousands of robots and worth some ten million credits on any world in the Galaxy—and no questions asked.

Old Brennmeyer had planned the whole thing. He had planned it for thirty years and more. It had been his life's work.

"It's the getaway, young man," he had said. "That's why I need you. You can lift a ship off the ground and out into space. I can't."

"Getting it into space is no good, Mr Brennmeyer," Trent said. "We'll be caught in half a day."

"Not," said Brennmeyer, craftily, "if we make the Jump; not if we flash through and end up light-years away."

"It would take half a day to plot the Jump and even if we could take the time, the police would alert all stellar systems."

"No, Trent, no." The old man's hand fell on his, clutching it in trembling excitement. "Not all stellar systems, only the dozen in our neighbourhood. The Galaxy is big and the colonists of the last fifty thousand years have lost touch with each other."

He talked avidly, painting the picture. The Galaxy now was like the surface of man's original planet (Earth, they had called it) in prehistoric times. Man had been scattered over all the continent, but each group had known only the area immediately surrounding itself.

"If we make the Jump at random," Brennmeyer said, "we would be anywhere, even fifty thousand light-years away, and there would be no more chance of finding us than a pebble in a meteor swarm."

Trent shook his head. "And we don't find ourselves either. We wouldn't have the foggiest way of getting to an inhabited planet."

Brennmeyer's quick-moving eyes inspected the surroundings. No one was near him, but his voice sank to a whisper anyway. "I've spent thirty years collecting data on every habitable planet in the Galaxy. I've searched all the old records. I've travelled thousands of light-years, farther than any space-pilot. And the location of every habitable planet is now in the memory store of the best computer in the world."

Trent lifted his eyebrows politely.

Brennmeyer said, "I design computers and I have the best. I've also plotted the exact location of every luminous star in the Galaxy, every star of spectral class of F, B, A, and O, and put that into the memory store. Once we've made the Jump the computer will scan the heavens spectroscopically and compare the results with the map of the Galaxy it contains. Once it finds the proper match, and sooner or later it will, the ship is located in space and it is then automatically guided through a second Jump to the neighbourhood of the nearest inhabited planet."

"Sounds too complicated."

"It can't miss. All these years I've worked on it and it can't miss. I'll have ten years left yet to be a millionaire. But you're young; you'll be a millionaire much longer."

"When you Jump at random. you can end inside a star."

"No one chance in a hundred trillion, Trent. We might also land so far from any luminous star that the computer can't find anything to match up against its programme. We might find we've jumped only a light-year or two and the police are still on our trail. The chances of that are smaller still. If you want to worry, worry that you might die of a heart attack at the moment of take-off. The chances for that are much higher."

"You might, Mr Brennmeyer. You're older."

The old man shrugged. "I don't count. The computer will do everything automatically."

Trent nodded and remembered that. One midnight, when the ship was ready and Brennmeyer arrived with the Krillium in a brief-case (he had no difficulty, for he was a greatly trusted man). Trent took the briefcase with one hand while his other moved quickly and surely.

A knife was still the best, just as quick as a molecular depolariser, just as fatal, and much more quiet. Trent left the knife there with the body, complete with fingerprints. What was the difference? They wouldn't get him.

Deep in space now, with the police-cruisers in pursuit, he left the gathering tension that always preceded a Jump. No physiologist couldn't could explain it, but every space-wise pilot knew what it felt like.

There was a momentary inside-out feeling as his ship and himself for one moment of non-space and non-time, became non-matter and non-energy, then reassembled itself instantaneously in another part of the Galaxy.

Trent smiled. He was still alive. No star was too close and there were thousands that were close enough. The sky was alive with stars and the pattern was so different that he knew the Jump had gone far. Some of those stars had to be spectral class F and better. The computer would have a nice, rich pattern to match against its memory. It shouldn't take long.

He leaned back in comfort and watched the bright pattern of starlight move as the ship rotated slowly. A bright star came into view, a really bright one. It didn't seem more than a couple of light years away and his pilot's sense told him it was a hot one; good and hot. The computer would use that as its base and match the pattern centred about it. Once again, he thought: It shouldn't take long.

But it did. The minutes passed. Then an hour. And still the computer clicked busily and its lights flashed.

Trent frowned. Why didn't it find the pattern? The pattern had to be there. Brennmeyer had showed him his long years of work. He couldn't have left out a star or recorded it in the wrong place.

Surely stars were born and died and moved through space

while in being, but these changes were slow, slow. In a million years, the patterns that Brennmeyer had recorded couldn't—

A sudden panic clutched at Trent. No! It couldn't be. The chances for it were even smaller than jumping into a star interior.

He waited for the bright star to come into view again, and, with trembling hands, brought it into telescopic focus. He put in all the magnification he could, and around the bright speck of light was the tell-tale fog of turbulent gases caught, as it were, in mid-flight.

It was a noda!

From dim obscurity, the star had raised itself to bright luminosity-perhaps only a month ago. It had graduated from a special class low enough to be ignored by the computer, to one that would be most certainly taken into account.

But the nova that existed in space didn't exist in the computer's memory store because Brennmeyer had not put it there. It had not existed when Brennmeyer was collecting his data—at least not as a luminous star.

"Don't count on it," shrieked Trent. "Ignore it."

But he was shouting at automatic machinery that would match the nova-centred pattern against the Galactic pattern and find it nowhere and continue, nevertheless, to match and match and match for as long as its energy supply held out.

The air supply would run out much sooner. Trent's life would ebb away much sooner.

Helplessly, Trent slumped in his chair, watching the mocking pattern of star light and beginning the long and agonised wait for death.

—If he had only kept the knife.

译后记

常常有初涉翻译的同学问我,做好翻译需要哪些过程?其实,这跟做其他学术研究也没有什么不同,无非还是那"三板斧"——理论、历史、实践。具体到翻译上,就是翻译理论,包括具有描述、解释、预测功能的纯翻译理论,以及指导功能的应用翻译理论,具有借鉴功能的翻译史,还具有实用功能的翻译实践。

法国哲学家帕斯卡说过:"智慧胜于知识。"如果说,知识回答的"是什么",那么,智慧回答的就是"怎么样"和"为什么"。对于翻译来说,翻译理论和翻译史解决的是宏观层面"何为译"的问题;文化,特别是语言对比解决的是"译何为"的问题;从语法、逻辑、修辞三个维度审视翻译实践解决"如何译"的问题。当然,翻译是一个需要 know something about everything 的专业,也就是"you don't need to know everything about something, but you need to know a little bit of everything",掌握一些翻译辅助工具也很有必要。

对于翻译理论,我曾在专著《翻译基础指津》(中译出版社,2017年)中有过专题阐述,这里就不再赘述,说到底,科学的核心是理论,没有理论,你的研究将一无所有。

对于翻译理论与实践之间的关系，要明确的是离开实践的理论是空洞的理论，离开理论的实践是盲目的实践。

翻译是一种看似门槛很低、实则难度很高的学术。其实，不是学语言的都是学英语的；不是学英语的都能做翻译；不是做翻译的什么文体都能翻译。相对于母语创作来说，翻译创作的难度更高。对于英语专业来说，听说读写译，最难莫过于翻译；对于各种翻译文体来说，最难莫过于文学翻译。至于翻译标准，我觉得上下文，也只有上下文，才是决定词义、段义、句义、文义的唯一标准。这个上下文可以是上一个词和下一个词，也可以是上一句和下一句，或者是上一段和下一段，甚至是上一章和下一章，乃至同一作者所著的上一部作品和下一部作品。具体践行到中观层面，双语差异之处，便是困难之时。到了微观层面，译得通不通是语法问题，译得对不对是逻辑问题，译得好不好是修辞问题。

下面，就以之前翻译的图书为例，来做一简要的实证。

一、逻辑

例1. Do you understand what condoms are used for?
你知道安全套是用来做什么的吗？
——《谋杀的颜色》

（原文中被问的是一个14岁的孩子，所以condom虽然是一个专有名词，通常选择一个义项即可，但考虑到孩子对性的有限认知,这里只能译成"安全套",不能译成"避孕套"。)

例2. She had been older than he then in Ohio. Now she was not young at all. Bill was still young.

当年在俄亥俄州的时候她就比他大,现在,她毕竟已经不再年轻,而比尔却不见老。

——译趣坊第一辑《时光不会辜负有爱的人》之《初秋》

(原文 Bill was still young 是肯定形式,译文转换成了否定形式,但内容没有变,反而更为准确。)

例3. God made Coke, God made Pepsi, God made me, oh so sexy, God made rivers, God made lakes, God made you…well we all make mistakes.

上帝创造了可口可乐,上帝创造了百事可乐,上帝创造了我,哦,多么性感。上帝创造了河流,上帝创造了湖泊,上帝创造了你……怎么说呢,谁能不出错呢?

——译趣坊第一辑《人生是一场意外的遇见》之《毒舌段子》

(原文的 well we all make mistakes 译成了"怎么说呢,谁能不出错呢?"肯定变否定,句号变问号,但内在的逻辑始终如一。)

二、语法

例1. "Do you think all these people are happy with the wonderful things they have?" She asked.

"People happy with things? No, no," the old man said. "Only people make people happy. You just have to know how to love people. People aren't things; people think, they feel. You have to tell them you love them. You have to show them. You have to say nice things. You have to mean them…"

"你觉得这些拥有好东西的人幸福吗？"她问道。

"拥有东西的人幸福？不对，不对，"老人说道，"只有人才能让人幸福。你需要知道怎么去爱别人就够了。人不是东西；人会思考，人有感觉。你要告诉别人你爱他们，你要把爱展示给他们看。你要说金玉良言，要有真情实感……"

——译趣坊第一辑《愿你出走半生　归来仍是少年》之《幸福在哪里》

（关于一词多义，就是要"确认过眼神，选择对的含义"。原文的 wonderful things 在上下文中有哲学意味，指代的是物质，这里在讨论的实际上是物质和精神与幸福之间的关系，所以译成"东西"；You have to say nice things 里的 things 指的是话语，所以译成了"金玉良言"。）

例2. Saying goodbye in autumn is not saying goodbye forever.

对秋天说再见，秋天还会见。

——《英汉经典阅读系列散文卷》之《乡村之秋》

（关于句法翻译，要分析原文的句子成分，先找出主谓宾，然后找出定状补，确定句意。双语能"神同步"真真是极好的。不能就或分或合，或缩或扩，或换序，或变性、变态，甚至十八般武艺并用，舍"形"而取"义"。从语言层次的转换情况来看，既可以是同一层次的同类型转换，也可以是同一层次的非同类型转换，还可以是超越同一层次的转换。从本句来看，译文做了分句处理，属于同一类型的非同类型转换。）

例3. I loved you enough to accept you for what you are, not what I wanted you to be.

我爱你至深，才接受你现在的样子，尽管不是我期望的样子。

——译趣坊第一辑《时光不会辜负有爱的人》之《爱你至深》

（关于从句翻译，原文的 what you are 和 what I wanted you to be 实现了从句译成词组，句型由抽象向具体的转换。）

例4. They are hard to find when your eyes are closed, but they are everywhere you look when you choose to see.

选择合上双眼，天使很难发现；选择睁大双眼，天使会在任何地方出现。

——译趣坊第二辑《生命中一直在等待的那一天》之《天使何所似》

（英文重形合，句子成分"一个都不能少"，所以连词、关系词、介词多，译成汉语，很多时候，一省了之。原文的 when 和 but 就是如此。）

例5. "You're a very good dancer," she sighed.

"你的舞跳得好好啊！"她叹道。

——译趣坊第三辑《愿我们每个人都被世界温柔以待》之《下雨天，留人天》

（在翻译过程中，英汉两种语言的词类或词性均会经常发生转换。没有什么词是不能"变性"的，本句原文的名词 dancer 就译成了动词"跳"。从本质上讲，汉语是一种多运用动词的语言，是真正的"动感地带"。）

三、修辞

例1. Alarmed, sad? He smiled, and his smile kept on getting broader, and before long, he was dissolving into laughter. He was determined to control himself, but this resistance collapsed completely. He started guffawing loudly…

感到奇怪？难过？他微微笑着，接着，嘴越咧越大，迸发出一声大笑，他想自控，但这一抵抗立刻土崩瓦解了，竟哈哈大笑不止。

——译趣坊第一辑《愿你出走半生 归来仍是少年》之《幸福的人》

（这是层递修辞格，程度递增，直译过来，一目了然。）

例2. May you always walk your path with love. May you always help your fellow travelers along the way. And may your roads always lead you Home again.

愿你的人生之路都有爱为伴，愿你在旅途中帮助同路人，愿你人生中的一段又一段旅程都是通往回"家"的路。

——译趣坊第二辑《所有的路　最终都是回家的路》之《所有的路，最终都是回家的路》

（这是重复修辞格，译文三个"愿你"，一一对应，句句对应，原文 roads 的复数得到强化翻译，作为全篇收尾的画龙点睛之笔。）

例 3. Even more than what they eat I like their intellectual grasp. It is wonderful. Just watch them read. They simply read all the time.

我喜欢他们的饮食，但是我更喜欢他们学富五车。那真是了不起。看看他们看的书就一目了然了。他们简直就是手不释卷。

——译趣坊第三辑《如果事与愿违　请相信一定另有安排》之《怎样成为百万富翁》

（修辞翻译也可以"无中生有"，本句中的 intellectual grasp 译成"学富五车"、read all the time 译成"手不释卷"，也都毫无违和感。）

例 4. Neither manifested the least disposition to retreat. It was evident that their battle-cry was "Conquer or die".

双方都没有一丝一毫的退却表现，显然他们的战争口号是"不成功便成仁"。

——译趣坊第三辑《选一种姿态　让自己活得无可替代》之

《红蚂蚁大战黑蚂蚁》

（修辞可以让你的译文变得更有腔调。"想要有腔调，就不能说大白话，得加上装饰"。原文中的 Conquer or die 是一个仿拟修辞格，以归化的策略套译成"不成功便成仁"，来描绘双方死战的状态，成为亲切的"中国风"。）

Language is shaped by, and shapes, human thought. 这句话的意思是"人的思想形成语言，而语言又影响了人的思想。"文学翻译是一个在各美其美、美人之美的基础上，力争美美与共的过程。原作者的思想形成了原作者的语言，原作者的语言又影响了我的思想。文学翻译让我意识到：文学的终极使命，是一种灵魂的救赎，我庆幸自己此生在一个不合时宜的时空做了一件不合时宜的事情，它唤醒了我心中一个蠢蠢欲动的自己。我爱这个自己，我相信文学"他者"的魔力，可以让一只匍匐的虫豸，陡然生出纵横天地的心，化茧成蝶。

让"译趣坊系列"也带你飞。

张白桦

2020 年大暑于塞外古城